The Lic

C000175077

Eva Leon

Chapter 1 - Chris

New beginnings are always an exciting time. Chris Robertson didn't have many of them, but the few he'd managed to rack up in his life were always some of the most memorable. It was with this sense of anticipation that he was now headed for his first job straight out of college.

"I'm really lucky to have landed a position at LeoTech," Chris said into his Bluetooth.

Jeremy Robertson chuckled in his ear. "Sounds like all those long nights you pulled to get top marks in your coursework paid off. But you don't have to rush into this, Chris. Take your time and make sure you've examined all your options for employment."

Chris smiled to himself. His foster father meant well. He really appreciated all that Jeremy and his partner, Colin, had done for him when he was just a child. Being alone in the foster system had a way of grinding people down, and it was through the generosity of those parents who wanted to do something to help that Chris was now in his car, driving to his first official position after graduating college with honors in marketing.

"I know," Chris said. "I know it's going to be harder as an Omega to make my place in life, but I can't go back to that place. It is still too painful. I want to be able to hold my own, knowing one day I can give my family the things they need and want and not get trapped in the crushing cycle of poverty."

He had been trapped in that cycle for all of his childhood. It was only through the intervention of child services, after the repeated overdoses of his mother and unsuccessful attempts to find the father, that Chris was pulled from that. Placed with Jeremy and Colin, a mated pair of lion shifters, Chris finally found a home.

He never forgot where he came from, though. Never. The memories, somewhat tempered by time, still haunted him.

Chris vowed to never do that to his family.

"You know Colin and I support you, whatever you do," Jeremy said. Jeremy's Alpha nature was starting to shine through, although Chris could tell he was trying his best to keep a lid on it. "We will worry about you, Chris. You carry so much responsibility for things that you had no control over. Don't put too much undue pressure on yourself to succeed. That you

2

graduated and you've moved to your own apartment says a lot about your drive."

"I'll be fine, Jeremy," Chris said with a laugh. The concern of his foster parents, certainly more than his real parents ever gave him, was the impetus of what kept him moving forward and not crumpling beneath the weight of his pain as he grew up.

With hard work and a lot of self-help books, Chris had finally been able to put most of his memories to rest. That didn't mean he wasn't acutely aware of the sins of his past.

He merged into the middle of the five lanes of traffic heading at breakneck speed towards the downtown area. "I hate to hang up," Chris said as he darted between two cars, carefully matching speed, "but I'm starting to hit heavy traffic. Tell Colin I promise to come home once a month."

"Alright, son. He'll probably insist on coming to see your new apartment before then. I'll have him get in touch. You know how he gets. Good luck today. I'm sure you'll crush it."

Chris ended the call so he could focus on the rhythm of brake lights. He checked his watch. He made sure to leave the apartment in plenty of time to get to the new job after a few test runs. Leaving anything to chance was not an option. He would have left at 4 a.m. if it meant he would be on time.

Provided there were no accidents to block even one lane, he should arrive at the office building with twenty minutes to spare.

Once he was settled into the traffic pattern, he watched as the tall buildings of the downtown area slowly grew in size on the horizon.

His conversation with Jeremy was just one of many they'd had after Chris graduated. Both his foster fathers were worried he was going to rush through life on some mythical race for success. Colin was especially worried Chris would be so focused on the race that he would forget that all the stress that comes with chasing success means nothing without a family for support.

Chris smiled to himself. He believed that was Colin's way of saying *don't forget this family.* As if Chris ever could forget everything Colin and Jeremy had done for him. They truly were more of a family for him than his mother ever had been.

He wasn't sure how to reassure them that he knew the prize his eyes were on. Family was great, but it wasn't fair to them if he couldn't provide for them. The culmination of his dream was to be a good provider.

Then, one day, he'd find an Alpha who had no problems with an Omega partner having a fulfilling career to build a family and a life with.

***

Chris was doubly fortuitous that he had mapped and timed his route before his start date. He was able to score some decent parking in the parking garage across the street from the building.

A glance at his watch indicated he had some time before he needed to report to HR. Deciding not to take the skyway bridge across the major avenue that cut through the downtown area and separated parking from work, Chris headed to the street level in the hunt for some coffee.

He lucked out. The coffee cart at the corner of the block wasn't but a short jog to the entrance to LeoTech. It was basic offerings of coffee and some plain pastries. After a brief decision to *not* risk eating something sugary on his nervous stomach, he queued up.

Never losing sight of his watch and how much time he had.

He didn't go through all this just to end up delayed at the coffee cart.

Chapter 2 - Landon

"Mr. Williams."

The sultry voice of Caroline King, LeoTech's VP of HR, called out behind Landon as he left the Monday morning staff meeting. He debated the wisdom of letting her know he heard her or simply racing for the elevator without *looking* like he was trying to escape.

"Landon, seriously...I know you're thinking about trying to run."

He paused, sighed deeply, and pivoted on one heel. He dragged the leather jacket draped over his shoulder to rest it over a forearm and shoved a hand into his jeans pocket. There was even a moment of consideration on whether to remove his sunglasses, but far too many tequilas the night before still made his sight a bit sensitive to the light.

Not that Caroline would tolerate that bit of disrespect. She could be a hard-ass when she had something on her mind, like she clearly did right at this moment.

He pushed his glasses up to rest on top of his head. "Good morning, Caroline."

She came to a stop in front of him and waved a stack of file folders. "We have some new hires coming in this morning. I thought it would be a nice touch for you to address them as CEO." Her hand fell away and she gave him the once-over, judgment evident on her face.

Landon looked down at the way he was dressed. "What?"

"It's hardly a professional look for the office."

She was right. If he gave a shit about it, it might actually bother him. He wasn't about to let it get to him. "I hired competent VPs to run the business, Caroline, so I *didn't* have to come in and micromanage the company. I thought everyone was generally okay with this arrangement. I don't come in and tell people how to do what they're paid to do, they get to do what they're paid to do. Everyone goes home happy."

Caroline folded her arms and rocked on the heels of her Prada pumps. "Did it occur to you that occasionally we need the face of our company to put in an appearance—"

"Why do you think I'm here?"

"—in more appropriate office attire. I know you can afford a suit. I suspect you even have one tucked away in a box in your closet."

Landon eyed her. "I might."

"Then consider pulling it out every so often and using it when you come in to work."

"You'll want me to shave, too?"

"A haircut might be in order."

He held his hand up. "Now you've crossed the line."

"Then run a brush through it." Caroline's lip quirked up as she fought her smile. Yeah, she came across as a battle-axe but she was one of his first VP hires and he never had reason to regret it. Even when she was busting his chops over his long hair.

"You just enjoy the smell of Vitalis."

That broke her and she laughed out loud. With a wave of her folders, she headed down the hall that led toward HR. "God, you're such a jerk. Seriously, it wouldn't hurt for you to stick your unshaven, unbrushed head in the orientation meeting so they actually *know* what their boss looks like?"

"You're walking away, which means you're resigned to the fact that I won't."

"Don't forget there's a board meeting later this month. You definitely need to show up for that in a suit."

"I'll dig it out if I can find it!" he shouted behind her as she entered HR. She flapped the folders at him before the door swung shut behind her.

With a smirk, he pulled his sunglasses down again and headed to the elevator.

***

He wasted no time crossing the lobby and finally stepping outdoors into the early morning sun. Pausing, Landon gave his eyes a moment to adjust to the light, even though they were protected by the shades. The cheerfully sunny day did nothing for the slight hangover he was sporting, but being out of the building, even though city air could hardly be called fresh, was a balm to his soul.

Landon Williams, CEO of LeoTech Industries, *hated* being cooped up in a soulless box. Much less chained to a desk.

That was why he put all the time, energy and expense into hiring the sharpest individuals and putting them in positions of authority in his company. It operated like a well-oiled machine that required little maintenance.

Contrary to what Caroline wanted to believe, Landon *did* keep tabs on the company. He wasn't completely hands-off, but he put great effort in the appearance of being hands-off.

It was his super power.

A breeze swirled down the main avenue, picking up litter that hadn't made it into the garbage bins and ruffling the edges of the vendor cart umbrellas shielding its early morning patrons. On the breeze, Landon caught something. A whiff.

The scent of something that stirred the primal beast lodged deep within him.

His Alpha lion nature.

Pulling his glasses off, he squinted against the glare as he looked for the source. Another deep inhale gave him a better idea of distance and direction. It came from someone in the line at the coffee cart.

His nose, filled with the scent of another lion, an *Omega*, caused him a moment of disorientation. On automatic, he moved to the line. His instinct, guided by the scent, led him right to the current object of his attention.

The guy was young. Couldn't be more than twenty-three or twenty-four years old. His light brown hair ruffled in the continued breeze that picked up his scent and tormented Landon. He stood just a head shorter than Landon, slighter build. His shoulders were broad and fit without being overly muscular, but it was the way his back and waist tapered to slim hips. The slacks he wore showed off the most perfect ass Landon had laid eyes on in…hell, he didn't know how long.

His young prey was very well put together. With every deep inhale, it was driving Landon crazier to get to know the body that stood in front of him.

He leaned in to the younger man. "Hey."

The guy jumped, as if he hadn't been expecting Landon to be there. That wasn't true, and Landon knew it. The guy was an Omega and Landon was an Alpha. The Omega knew exactly who he was.

It probably shouldn't be so cute to be jumpy, but it was to Landon. Almost like he was new to the city.

"Maybe it's presumptuous of me," Landon said, still leaning down to talk in the Omega's ear, "but something tells me you're new."

The guy glanced nervously over his shoulder. Their eyes met and it felt like Landon had rammed his finger in a light socket. Then, that sweet, pink tongue swept out to wet his lips in a move that threatened to drive Landon out of his damn mind.

"I am. Sort of."

"Sort of," Landon repeated. He straightened, looked up at the menu board on the cart, then leaned down again. "Then let me buy you a cup of coffee."

The scent of arousal coming from this little Omega was intense. Landon considered himself very lucky to have run across this tasty morsel of a man. There had to be a way to get this one into bed with him.

The line progressed and the Omega stepped up to the window. He leaned in to quietly order and shoved money across to the vendor. "Thanks. But I have to go. Have a good morning."

And just like that, the Omega was pushing through the crowd to disappear into Landon's office building.

Dude just rebuffed his advances. Landon couldn't remember the last time he was turned down for *anything*. Instead of feeling defensive, he was surprisingly intrigued by this turn of events.

With a grin, Landon ordered his coffee and slid his sunglasses back down on his face.

Oh yeah. Challenge accepted, little Omega.

Chapter 3 - Chris

Getting in the building was Chris's first priority.

It wasn't that he was skeeved out by the Alpha hitting on him. Quite the contrary, actually.

The presence of the Alpha had that cloying, closed effect on Chris. He needed the distance. Hormones were playing merry hell with his ability to see straight and having the Alpha all but on top of him had him swaying. His vision was blurred and whiting out from the sheer desire that swamped him.

Chris didn't even know the guy!

Once he got inside the building, Chris paused to stare out the darkened lobby windows at the crowd around the coffee cart.

The Alpha was still there. He pulled some money from his front pocket and swiped up his coffee. Now his glasses were over his eyes. It didn't stop the feeling that he was looking right at Chris.

Startled, Chris stepped back, turning quickly to head straight for the crowd assembled at the elevator.

Even in the crowd, Chris felt the presence of the man. It was disconcerting.

It was hard to fight his instincts to keep glancing at the revolving door. Chris half expected the Alpha to prowl in behind him.

Images unbidden came to mind of being trapped in the elevator and having the Alpha take him right there.

He shook his head and glanced over his shoulder as casually as he could, sipping on his coffee until, thankfully, the ding announced the elevator and the doors slid open. When Chris finally stepped in the elevator, his fear that the Alpha would follow him into the building finally went away. The safety of the door closing giving Chris that extra sigh of relief.

Maybe a little disappointment. Only a little.

Tucking himself in the far corner, Chris kept his attention straight ahead, watching as the floor level indicators illuminated. The elevator car moved slowly as it stopped to let some passengers disembark and take on more. The higher he went, the fewer people remained in there with him, the blessed silence giving him the cocoon he needed to gather his nerves and try to put that gorgeous Alpha out of his mind.

It wasn't that easy. Sure, the guy was amazingly well put together. Hey, Chris was able to get a glimpse of him after he escaped inside the building so he took the opportunity. Long blond hair and those amazing golden eyes.

The scent of his Alphaness had almost buckled Chris's knees. It was enough to make him slick with heady arousal.

But the guy looked like he couldn't afford a cup of coffee, much less next month's rent.

The elevator car grew uncomfortably close as it neared his floor. When it dinged, Chris bolted out like a shot, stopping just short of the reception area so he could catch his breath.

Even though he was standing in the open, he felt the phantom warmth at his back as the Alpha leaned in. He *towered* over Chris and it gave him a little thrill to know someone that intensely *Alpha*, who he didn't know, was interested.

Interested in *sex*, sure, but interested all the same.

It punched all his kink buttons and he swallowed a gulp of his coffee to stifle the purr of contentment that threatened to vibrate right out of him. That really didn't need to happen on his first day.

Now that he'd gotten some coffee in him, he disposed of his half empty cup and stepped up to the reception desk. "Hi," he said after clearing his throat nervously. "I'm Chris Robertson. A new hire."

The receptionist looked up from where he was writing out a call message and he smiled up at Chris. After a moment's scrutiny, he shuffled through some papers before stuffing them into a file and handing them out to Chris, along with a guest badge. "To your left and down the hall. Follow the signs to the new hire orientation. Welcome to LeoTech."

"Thanks." Chris took the folder and headed to the conference room.

By the time he got there, two other people were there. At the end of the table was a small breakfast tray and four carafes. As if on cue, his stomach gurgled and he smiled shyly as it seemed to echo around the room.

He grabbed some water from the pitcher next to the spread and a bagel with cream cheese and found a place not too far from one of the new hires already sitting there with a half-eaten donut. She had curly red hair and cute freckles that dotted over the bridge of her nose. She gave him a wide grin and stuck her hand out. "I think I like this place already if they feed us breakfast. I'm Clarissa."

Chris took her hand and settled in the chair next to her. "I'm Chris. I am so glad they have it. I forgot to eat breakfast this morning. Do they do this for regular employees?"

The guy sitting across from him was wearing a very nice fitting suit. Chris was suddenly seized with the fear that maybe he was underdressed. The Suit nodded his head. "I have a friend who works in R&D and he says every Monday they treat employees for breakfast."

"Is that where you're going, Rich?" Clarissa asked.

"Yeah. My buddy, he got me a job working in their QA section. Testing and stuff like that. I'm Rich." He leaned across the table to shake hands with Chris. "Where are you going?"

"Marketing." Chris realized they hadn't split the bagels and sawing it in two with the plastic knife was going to make a mess. He settled for breaking off pieces and using the knife to put the cream cheese on each bite.

They made small talk about the traffic and where they parked. Apparently, working for the company would entitle them to free parking if you were lucky enough to score the lottery drawing for it. Chris filed that away. Since his apartment wasn't so far away that Uber was out of his price range, he considered that option if paying for parking became too prohibitive.

In the middle of Rich's map for the optimum route to get to the office building and avoid a major exchange from the bypass, a woman in impossibly high heels sailed into the room. Her hair was perfectly quaffed and was a bright blonde. "Good morning, everyone. We are expecting a couple more people who are running late but there's no reason why we can't get started."

The receptionist Chris had seen out front was assisting her as she passed out pens and more forms.

"My name is Caroline King and I'm head of HR. This smiling gentleman," and she gestured to the receptionist, "is Stan Rollins. He's the smiling face of LeoTech Industries. If you have any questions, you can ask him and he'll direct you where you need to go."

Stan smiled and lifted a hand.

"While we wait for our stragglers, we'll get started on the necessary forms."

**

Chris had never worked at a place where their orientation took up most of the morning. After the last of the review of the employee handbook, the new hires were split off to meet their supervisors and the heads of their departments before lunch.

Caroline walked beside Chris as they headed for the marketing section. "So, now that you've been through the worst of it, Chris, how do you feel about working here? Do you have any questions?"

Chris gave her a wide-eyed look. "Hard to say, Mrs. King. It's a lot to take in."

"Well, inside the front cover of your handbook is the HR portal website. That's where we have all the rules and regulations posted, as well as contact names for most of the key people. And if all else fails—"

"Call Stan," they said together.

She laughed along with him. "You can't go wrong."

Stopping in front of a wood door, she rapped on it twice. Waiting for the muffled invitation to go in, she motioned for Chris to follow. "Shawn, I have your new marketing hire. This is Chris Robertson. Chris, this is Shawn Torres, VP of Marketing." She handed Shawn a file folder before turning to Chris. "I leave you in his capable hands."

Shawn waited for Caroline to leave before he motioned for Chris to sit. He flapped the folder on the desk. "The most grueling part of your day is over. Good God, new hire orientation has got to be *the* most boring presentation to sit through."

Chris smoothed a nervous hand over the back of his head. "It wasn't too bad but the room was kind of stuffy."

Shawn picked up the phone and spoke into it briefly before addressing Chris. "Well, you're free now."

Moments later, there was a knock. Chris turned to see a man poke his head in the door. "Hey, Shawn. You needed to see me?"

Shawn waved him in. "Buzz, this is Chris. He's new. Chris, I'm putting you with Buzz to get set up and get your feet under you."

Chris followed Buzz for the tour of the marketing division and meeting the people he would be working with. After a while, their names started to get jumbled together and Chris was relieved when Buzz stopped in front of an obviously vacant desk. He was positive he wouldn't remember anyone's name.

"IT hasn't shown up with your computer," Buzz said apologetically. "They said some time around lunch. So if you want to have a seat and test run the drawers, you should find a pen and paper in there somewhere. Make a list of office supplies and we'll hit the supply closet after lunch, then go get your ID badge. Here's your extension number and the instructions on how to program your voicemail." Buzz pointed to the number on the front of the phone instruction book before handing it over to Chris.

"What time is lunch?"

"Right now, actually. There's a restaurant on the eighth floor and a lot of fast places within walking distance. And of course, the food carts if you're feeling brave." Buzz glanced at his watch. "So...want to meet back here at one-fifteen?"

"That sounds good," Chris glanced around the desk, his hand smoothing over the surface. He was trying to fight the feeling he was utterly overwhelmed.

Apparently Buzz saw his expression and laughed. "Everyone is like that when they first get here. By the end of the week, you'll be an old hat. See you in an hour."

Chris watched as Buzz disappeared. The sudden sinking feeling that he was out of his depth washed over him like a wave.

He stood from the desk and glanced for the door to take him to the elevators.

First-day nerves sucked.

Chapter 4 - Landon

Sure, there were plenty of places for Landon to be, but his life got a whole lot more interesting running into that sweet little Omega. Now, he didn't exactly have proof, at least not yet, but he suspected that Omega was working for his company. LeoTech Industries owned the building, after all. There were a few startups that leased space, and there was a chance the guy was working for one of them. He had that look, after all.

Young, energetic, eager. It was in his bearing, even when he was running from Landon.

It was his scent that intrigued Landon the most. It affected him on a very deep level. More than sexual interest, although there was plenty of that.

It had him waiting around the downtown area for lunch, betting on the fact that the Omega would escape the building to look for something to eat.

He parked his bike along the street and pulled out his phone to do some reading, play a few games of Sudoku and feed the meter until the lunch hour.

Patience?

Landon could have patience when he wanted to. Waiting out this Omega was one of those times. He was positive he'd see the guy.

And...right on cue, ten minutes past the hour, out walked the Omega, glancing around as if to get his bearings.

His pride swelled that he managed to call this right. Not that there was any doubt, but sometimes people could be unpredictable. Not this time, however.

He paused his game and stuffed his phone in his pocket to go talk to the Omega.

The young guy turned and his gaze landed right on Landon. A brief look of panic crossed his face and he stepped back. Just as quickly, he ducked his head, swiveled on a heel and started walking briskly. It was kind of cute.

Landon jogged up and fell into step with him. "Hey again."

The Omega glanced up and muttered a soft "Hey." His pace didn't slow. They walked at damn near a jog.

He almost laughed. His instincts cautioned him against it. "Look, could you slow down a moment so we can talk?"

"I don't have long for lunch," the guy said, gesturing to his watch.

"You have an hour."

That brought a surprised look from the guy, who stopped suddenly. It caused Landon to pivot quickly and come to a stop in front of him. "Look…" the Omega's gaze darted around as if he was looking for something. "I…"

Landon pushed his glasses up and he held his hands out. "You think I'm stalking you?" He had to fight down another laugh but it didn't stop his smile. "I promise I'm not. Honestly. I just…you look like you could use a friend, and I could be a friend. I know what you are and I know you know what I am. So yeah, I'm a little interested, but I'm not going to pull an asshole move or anything."

The look of concern shifted subtly to one of disbelief. "And why would a stalker tell me he's not a stalker if he wasn't really a stalker?"

Landon's mouth opened and shut. "You're right. I guess you'll have to take my word for it. Do I look like a guy who would lie?"

The appraising look he got in return actually made him wonder for a brief moment if the guy would actually say yes.

"I don't know. No. I guess. But the best liars are those who don't look like liars."

"Wow. That's some hardcore mistrust you got going there."

"I am the one being followed."

"I'm not sure I have anything to say to that." Landon squinted up at the sun. "But it's lunch and the sun is getting hot. Can I at least take you to lunch?"

"I was going to get lunch at a vendor."

"Seriously? Some of the carts are really good. The guy across the street serves wonderful gyros but...do you eat Pad Thai? Because there's a great place just around the corner." Landon gestured.

For a moment, Landon thought the guy would say no. To his relief, the Omega nodded shortly. "Sure."

Why was he so relieved? It wasn't like there was a shortage of Omegas for Landon to chat up. What was different about this guy that he earnestly thought the guy needed to think well of him. He didn't want just *any* Omega. He wanted *this* one.

That was a change.

***

The wait wasn't long to get a small table against the outer window. The choice of tables was agreeable to the Omega, which pleased Landon. "So," he leaned in after they placed their drink orders. "Do you have a name, Oh Paranoid One?"

After a moment's thought, "Chris."

"Chris." Landon had to fight the desire to *literally* purr his name out.

"Do *you* have a name, Oh Stalker One?"

Landon burst out with a laugh. "Touché. Landon." He extended a hand across the table.

The moment Chris shook his hand, he knew the kind of man he was. A lot could be gleaned from a person's handshake.

The touch of his skin was warm, almost like it vibrated in Landon's grip. It wasn't too firm or too soft and they held the connection in just the right amount of time before Chris broke it off. Either Chris was a natural in business or he had been coached very well.

In any event, it impressed Landon. "So what do you do, Chris?"

"Marketing and sales."

Landon nodded, letting the silence linger to allow Chris to elaborate.

He didn't.

The waitress came with their drinks and took their order and Chris spoke only when absolutely necessary. Landon chatted up the waiter, Stacy, with his customary familiarity. She was his favorite waiter because she was damn good at her job. They bantered for a bit before she left to put their lunch order in and Landon was able to turn his attention back to Chris, who watched with interest.

"You come here a lot."

"Good observation."

"So you work around here?"

"Yeah," Landon said. "Not far, actually. At least when I am in the office."

"Telecommute?"

"Something like that."

"So, this is a new job for you?"

"Yeah."

Boring conversation was boring. Landon wanted to know more. He wanted to know all of Chris's thoughts and opinions and he was like a stone wall.

Landon leaned in, his elbows on the table. "Your answers are so evasive."

"Like yours aren't?" Chris said with narrowed eyes.

"You got me again. You said at the cart that you're new to the city."

Chris nodded. "I come from a smaller community about an hour north of here. I mean, I've been in the city a few times, but I rarely come down this far into the downtown district."

Interesting. At least Chris was opening up a little. "What do you do for fun?"

Chris shrugged, his fingers drawing interesting shapes on the condensation on his water glass. "Hiking, mostly. There wasn't a lot of time during college to do much more than study."

"I hear there's great hiking in the northeast part of the state." Landon sipped at his Coke. "I haven't been there since I was a kid. Are the Granger Falls still open to the public?"

"Yeah. They built a new viewing deck at the top."

Getting Chris to open up was like pulling rebar from set concrete. "There's a lot to do in the city. Things to try. If you're interested, I'd like to show you around. Give you a tour of the city from a resident's perspective."

Chris's glass paused as he lifted it to take a drink. "Show me around?"

"Yeah. You know, like a date, only less formal?"

"You're asking me out on a date?"

"That was the idea."

"And do what?"

Landon scrubbed at his face with a chuckle. "Take you to dinner. There's the symphony in the park, which is in season right now. There are shows to go see. Museums. The Science Exploratorium, the planetarium, the zoo and aquarium. And dining. Lots of restaurants, like the one at the top of the Forrester building..."

Chris's gaze dropped to the table, his mouth set as if he were considering it.

Stacy interrupted them by bringing their lunch, which was a blessing as it seemed to break Chris's train of thought.

"Look," Landon said. He pulled over a napkin and a pen from his leather jacket pocket. Scribbling on it, he slid it across the table. "That's my cell. Call me if you're interested. I can come pick you up or I can come meet you. I promise, Chris, I'm not a bad guy if you give me a chance."

Chris pulled the napkin from beneath Landon's fingers. He folded it neatly and tucked it into his shirt pocket. "I'll think about it."

"That's all I ask," Landon said. He pulled his bowl of noodles over to start eating.

Chris was going to be a tough nut to crack. Landon pulled out all his charms and it seemed to barely make a dent. He didn't like leaving lunch feeling this uncertain, but one thing he was positive about.

He wanted to see Chris again.

He just hoped that Chris wanted to see *him* again.

Chapter 5 - Chris

For the rest of the day, Chris tried his best to drag his focus away from the very odd lunch he had with his 'I'm-not-a-stalker' stalker, Landon. The Alpha was nice enough and he really seemed to be trying to get to know him.

It wasn't that Chris didn't trust Landon. Not completely.

It really was how all of it came about.

First, he had this Alpha all up in his personal space. Then, Chris found the guy waiting for him at lunch. Who did that for someone they didn't know? He didn't have that much experience in the dating arena and his experiences were confined to college. He knew the guys he went out with because they had classes together or saw each other at the library or at the dining hall.

Landon's direct approach not only caught Chris off guard, but aroused his suspicions.

Well, Landon aroused other things as well. Chris's caution was successfully more powerful than his attraction to the Alpha. For the moment.

If Landon continued his pursuit, would he have the strength of character not to completely succumb?

And would that be such a bad thing if he did?

Chris took a deep, cleansing breath in an attempt to keep his thoughts clear and focus on his new job.

Buzz was true to his word. IT had brought his computer and set him up so he could start work.

Shawn gave him some reports to review, but it was easy work and he finished it up earlier than he anticipated.

Taking the short break, Chris texted his extension number to his fathers, then called his brother, Max, to let him know that he'd gotten the job.

Of all his foster brothers, Chris and Max were the closest, probably because they were the newest to Jeremy and Colin's found family.

"Robertson," Max said into his phone.

"Hey, Max."

"Chris! I didn't recognize the phone number. I guess this is your work extension?"

"Yeah."

"How's the first day going?"

Chris related all the boring first day details. Max, recently at a new job of his own, commiserated with him.

"The nerves will be gone after about a week," Max advised.

"I hope so. Right now, the desire to not screw up is pretty high on the meter." Talking to Max was already bringing down his case of the nerves. "I wanted to talk to you about something weird that happened today. Do you have time?"

"I do. Hit me with it."

Chris explained to Max the events not only at the coffee cart, but lunch as well. He tried to keep it as neutral as possible so as not to taint his brother's opinion one way or the other. Max was very levelheaded. He would be able to cut through the smoke and mirrors quickly if there was something amiss.

After a pause, "I think you should do it."

What? Chris sat up in his chair. "Really? I don't know the guy. For all I know, he's homeless. Or broke. Or both. What if he wants to move in with me?"

Max let out an explosive laugh. "Move in with you? Chris? Dude, relax. You're a good-looking guy. It's natural that other guys into guys would find you attractive."

"Did I mention he's an Alpha? And he was in the business district in jeans and a leather jacket?"

"Was he greasy and smelly?"

Chris shifted in his seat when he immediately recalled the gorgeous mane of long blond hair. He remembered distinctly how much he wanted to run his hands through it. "No."

"So what is really bugging you, dude?"

"I just...don't want another deadbeat in my life."

"Ken was just a jerk, Chris. And when you saw his true colors, you had the good sense to dump his stupid ass fast. You've got the instincts. Go with them," Max said. "Besides, what do you have to lose? A free dinner with an extraordinarily hot guy? He was hot, right?"

Chris puffed out a breath. "Very."

"Right. He offered, so he'll pay. You have Jeremy's credit card for emergencies in case he deadbeats out of the bill, right? So, take a chance, eat on his dime, shake hands and go home. You don't have to take him *home* with you."

Chris chewed on his bottom lip in thought. Max did make sense.

"Chris—" Max's voice took on a serious tone. "I get you're worried. But you know how to keep yourself safe. You did it before Jeremy and Colin found you. Keep your wits about yourself and go out and enjoy the time in the city. Make friends. It'll do you good."

"Alright." Chris breathed out in determination. "And if I'm making a huge mistake, I'm blaming you."

Being in the city with no safety net was disconcerting and more than a little worrying. Max was right, though. He could get himself out of any trouble.

He just hoped he wasn't making a huge mistake.

Chapter 6 - Landon

Landon was in the middle of his lunch when he got the text from Chris about dinner. It came as a sweet surprise.

Sure, it was cute how Chris was actually attempting to resist his charms and everything. It began to dawn on Landon that he might have someone on his hands who was unaffected by them.

Not completely, of course. The Alpha-Omega pull was very strong in the shifter DNA, regardless of the species. In every one, it was instinctual. It took a strong will to resist it. Not all Omegas were able to, which was the main reason why Alphas like Landon never had a shortage of bed partners, when he was looking.

There was something different about Chris that kept Landon's attention. More than his being an Omega. He had spirit. It was low-key from what Landon had seen so far.

Even when Chris's text wasn't a home address, but to ask where they could meet. That was fire in Chris's spine. Chris was interested but he still wanted to play it safe.

Landon wanted to see more of that.

He thumbed in the name of the restaurant he had in mind and the time.

That, Landon would consider a minor victory.

Feeling quite pleased about it now, the giddy energy of excitement turned crazily in his gut. The excess energy had nowhere to go except to run it out.

Changing into slouch workout clothes, Landon headed for Chetham Park. If he was lucky, it wouldn't be crowded and he could run to his heart's content.

***

Finding easy parking beneath a tree, Landon hung his helmet on the bike handles and shook his hair out. He bungeed his jacket to the seat, confident that no one would try to walk off with it.

Chetham Park was the known local park refuge for shifters. It wasn't officially designated as such but the nonshifter population knew to steer clear.

Shifter-nonshifter relations in the city were good. Not fabulous, as not everyone thought shifters should be given the same rights as nonshifters. They were, thankfully, in the minority.

For the most part, everyone left each other alone, living in an easy, unofficial alliance.

They set aside Chetham Park as an oasis of safety for shifters to indulge in more of their animal natures.

Here, Landon could shift to his lion and run until pleasantly exhausted.

Starting at the edge of the park, Landon took off at a run. Each step took him to the wood line and closer to shifting. His body morphed beneath his skin, muscle and sinew and bone shifting to accommodate a new form. Soon two legs became four and Landon was racing through the woods, the scents of the city becoming more pronounced to his animal nose.

Lions were never built for prolonged running sprints but Landon was able to get up to top speed in record time as he sailed through the underbrush. Coming to an outcropping of rock, he slid to a stop, chest heaving from the running burst. Licking at his lips, he padded around the boulder and leaped up on it so he could get comfortable and feel the cool stone on his belly.

A gentle breeze blew through, bringing with it the scent of an Alpha lion nearby. Before he could place it, a body collided with him, taking him down off the rock. Both lions tumbled and rolled before Landon was able to gain his feet again.

His 'attacker' was a smaller lion, for relative sizes of Alphas. Where Landon's mane remained the same golden color of his hair when he was in human form, the intruding lion had a darker mane with heavy accents of black. Landon lifted his head and sniffed.

Clint Knowles.

Landon and Clint had an…uneasy relationship.

It wasn't friendship. It wasn't aggressive rivalry. It rested somewhere between on a sliding scale. Some days they got on, as most Alphas did. Some days, they butted heads as they competed for business or for lovers.

It wasn't hate, it wasn't like; Landon couldn't be sure if it was mutual respect either.

Perhaps, more like uneasy associates.

Clint shook his mane and bared his teeth in a roar. Not an aggressive challenge, more like a cocky taunt.

Landon got his footing and launched into a dead run at Clint, who got a late start in building up speed before they collided again. Landon's paw hooked into Clint's mane. As they sped past each other, Landon curled his paw and dragged Clint off balance. Clint was jerked off his paws and spun around in the grass right as Landon let him go.

Twigs, branches, grass and leaves kicked up as Clint rolled to his feet. He shifted form until he was standing as a human in front of Landon, the look of irritation very clear as he brushed his suit jacket off. He ran a hand through his mussed hair. "Williams. What brings you out here?"

Since Clint was in human form, Landon shifted as well. He strolled to recline against the rock, his fingers working out the twigs and leaves caught in his hair. "Same thing as you, I'd bet."

"I doubt that. I have no shortage of dates."

Landon scoffed. "Begging Omegas to go out with you hardly counts as a date, Knowles."

Clint smirked at Landon and flicked a small twig at him before wandering over to stand toe to toe. "At least they'll talk with me."

"Only because the superior Alpha has turned them away."

With a laugh, Clint glanced at his watch. "Don't you have some Judge Judy to watch or something?"

"Actually, I don't. I have better things to do with my time, and a delicious Omega to do them with."

"Well, it's not hard to imagine that when you clean up eventually *someone* would be desperate enough to say yes."

Egos were a weird thing. Landon normally didn't have that huge of an ego. Certainly not like Clint. Being around the other Alpha still managed to bring out the inner asshole in him. As if he *had* to match the man blow for blow just so Clint didn't get one up on him.

Clint had a chip on his shoulder. Landon's company was the top-rated tech firm, beating out Clint's by a wide profit margin. His share of the market was still the largest.

That was because Landon knew how to leave his developers and sales force the hell alone and let them do what they knew to do best.

Keep LeoTech at the top.

And Landon had weight and speed on Clint, both in human and in lion form.

Honestly, Landon was the better Alpha in all the ways that mattered.

"He'll be doing more than saying yes when I'm done," Landon preened cheekily.

Clint snorted softly but remained silent for a moment before he smiled, baring his teeth. "Care to go a round or two before you return to your pathetic life?"

Landon pushed up from his recline against the rock. "Only if you're ready to get your tail fed to you."

"You can try."

They separated and shifted to lion before turning to face each other.

As they circled, Landon paced calmly. He watched every bit of Clint. There was a playfulness to the way the other Alpha moved. Each sized the other up, looking for the ear flick, the tail twitch, the nostril flare that would telegraph their attack.

Eventually, Clint broke the standoff and raced at Landon. There was no real speed and when their bodies collided, no claws or teeth. Just a firm hold as they rolled and flipped before separating.

Another moment of measuring the opponent before they met in playfully aggressive holds to pull each other off balance.

Landon saw this for what it was. Every mock fight with Clint was with Clint's clear intent on gaining some insight into how Landon fought. He saw the writing on the wall. One day, they'd go at each other, with focused and present aggression to finally make this a true battle for the better Alpha.

Until then, Clint wasn't stupid enough to take on Landon in a real fight any time they found each other at the park. Mock fights were always playful, with that slight edge of conflict.

Sizing each other up for that one day.

And there would be a 'one day'.

Chapter 7 - Chris

Half a dozen times after agreeing to meet Landon for dinner, Chris almost canceled. He came very close a few times to texting the man and telling him something came up. He'd put his phone down with a frown. Lying didn't feel comfortable to him.

He had said yes and for a reason. He needed to see this through to the end. It was just one night and dinner, right?

That only lasted so long before Chris was distracted almost all the time with thoughts of Landon. The man was sinfully attractive. Just the few times Chris picked up the Alpha's scent, it turned his head around. Thoughts of Landon occupying all of his spare brain capacity was to the point it was distracting.

Chris did not need or want the sort of distraction Landon represented.

He really wasn't looking for a mate at all, if he were completely honest. This time in Chris's life, his timeline was getting established in his own career. Making it on his own and being beholden to no one. He wanted to do his foster fathers proud.

He wanted to do himself proud.

Making it on his own without the support of an Alpha was buried deep into his convictions.

Landon threatened that with his honey gaze and his golden hair.

Shawn cut him loose from the office early and Chris made good use of that time trying to find the right thing to wear. He didn't want to be pretentious and he didn't want to be too slouchy for the restaurant.

With Landon's casual style, he didn't want to be too overdressed either. The way Landon's jeans fit him was going to be distracting enough as it was.

Heaven squeezed into jeans, an Alpha scent that set Chris's head swimming and the topping like a cherry on a sundae was the knowledge that Landon wasn't just *any* Alpha but a lion Alpha. A perfect match for Chris.

No other Alpha than one who matched his species would understand Chris's desire to run through the wild with a perfectly suited mate. Nose to the wind, legs pumping with the exertion of a race through the woods.

Closing his eyes, Chris could see it. His traitorous body loved the idea of rolling in the grass with an Alpha lion, large paws batting playfully, his rough tongue grooming Chris's ear and cheek.

With a sigh, he glanced down at the raging hard-on that tented his underwear. He damn sure couldn't go out like that. And he definitely didn't need to meet Landon now, with all these sexy thoughts that could easily come up unbidden at any time.

His luck would be at the worst possible moment as well.

He stripped down and jumped in the cool water of a shower. The cool temperature beating against his erection brought a hiss from him, but cold water was not going to do the trick. There was only one way to handle this.

Easy enough to take care of. Just a quick stroke to take the top off the tension, that's all he needed.

Damn it all if the moment Chris shut his eyes, his imagination didn't helpfully supply him with the perfect stroke material. Immediately he could see Landon bending him over and plowing him thoroughly from behind. Sharp teeth scraping at the back of his shoulder in his fantasy were almost real to him, tingling along his skin as he ducked his head beneath the spray.

In the channel of his fist, Chris moved his hips to pump just to satisfy the need to move, to feel it physically. Light honey eyes and a mane of beautiful hair filled his vision until, startled, Chris painted the shower tile with his come.

As he stood there, shower pounding down over his head, Chris was only vaguely sated. Jerking off in solo action wasn't nearly as satisfying as if it happened with someone else. At least it did what he needed it to do — clear his head so he didn't spend the entire dinner wondering what it would feel like to have Landon's dick buried in his ass.

***

Chris stepped out of his Uber and waited for the car to pull from the curb before he headed for the restaurant's entrance. The dark wood portal was real wood, stained, not painted, with intricate carvings in the wooden door. Offset with a meticulously crafted stained glass window set in the door, the owners poured a lot of money into first impressions.

Piazza Navona was, according to Yelp, one of the best Italian gastropubs in the city. Casual dining with an impressively varied menu. They even served craft beer, which was Chris's weakness.

He loved local beer. That swill coming out of the big beer manufacturers was dreadful and no one could pay Chris enough to drink that nasty stuff. Nothing beat the home touch.

His brothers accused him of being a beer snob on more than one occasion. It was a moniker he would continue to wear with pride. At least it kept him in good beer.

So if the dinner proved to be a bust, Max was right. The food and the beer would be worth suffering through it.

Chris rubbed his palms along his slacks. Flashes of his fantasy from his shower threatened to come back on him. With a breath, he forcefully pushed those away. Chris was not a casual guy. When he had sex, he wanted it to have meaning. With someone like Landon, Chris just didn't see how that was possible.

Maybe Landon was a really nice guy. Chris couldn't consider even forming a casual bond with him.

It was clear they weren't for each other. Chris wanted more from an Alpha than a good lay. The Alpha he desired needed to be matched with him in other areas of his life.

A desire for a career and, at the risk of sounding like a gold digger, someone who was a little more financially stable. Chris had no desire in repeating the sins of his birth parents. He didn't want a deadbeat that he'd have to support.

No matter how attractive that deadbeat looked.

He had certain expectations of his life, and that included not stressing about money.

Two people pushed out the door before Chris could open it, forcing him to step back to let them pass. The rich aroma of Italian food wafted out and caused his stomach to growl. He wondered if Landon was already there. They had agreed on seven-thirty and Chris was ten minutes early.

The hostess at the podium greeted him with a smile. "Welcome to Piazza Navona. Party of one?"

"I'm actually supposed to meet someone here," Chris said. He glanced around the small dining area. It was hard to tell if he was more nervous that Landon would be there ahead of him or if he would be the one left waiting. In either scenario, the butterflies kicked up in his stomach. "Landon."

She glanced at her chart. "Right, he's already here. This way."

So Chris wasn't the first in. It was a good sign that Landon wasn't the sort to play games and make Chris wait long for him.

As they wove through the tables, Chris tried to keep his wits about him. Have dinner, maybe make a friend and that was as far as it would get. He wouldn't let himself get talked into dropping into bed with Landon and screwing up his entire plan for his life.

Eat, enjoy and go home. Maybe have another shower and jerk off one more time and then never do this again. God, what was he thinking? This was not a good idea.

Chris almost turned around when the hostess turned a corner and he saw Landon sitting at the table. Two beers sat on the table, one was in Landon's hands, the other sat at the place setting.

Landon stood when Chris approached. The hostess dropped the menus on the table and told them the server would be with them shortly, but Chris faintly heard her.

He was too busy fighting the rising instinct of submitting to the delicious Alpha who leaned in to kiss his cheek. Chris fought the desire to lean into Landon and breathe in his scent. The touch of Landon's hand as it slid down Chris's arm was warm and it lingered long after Landon pulled away and motioned for Chris to sit. He swallowed thickly, hoping the desire to purr at being so close to Landon went unheard.

All that crap about wanting more in his life? Someone more evenly matched?

Screw standards.

Chapter 8 - Landon

After his mock fight with Clint, Landon worked to overcome his annoyance at having run into the asshole when he was looking to reduce his nervousness.

Instead, he replaced nervousness with irritation. Fat lot of good going for a run in the park did.

He did want to shake it, though, and pressed the issue in his mind to cast off the negatives and focus on the positives.

Like how damn good Chris looked when Landon spotted him following the waitress, who led him right to his table. His choice of clothing was very stylish for the setting and Chris looked right at home. Chris obviously had good taste. That said nothing about how damn well Chris was put together. His slacks were well fitted and his torso tapered to a trim waist that looked tight. Yeah. Chris was going to fit right in here.

This was why Landon chose the Piazza Navona as their meeting place. His instincts said that Chris would be most comfortable there. Time would tell if Landon's instincts were right, but he had a good feel for this.

"I took the liberty of ordering you a beer," he said when Chris was close enough. He rose and pressed a tender kiss at the corner of Chris's jawbone. Being that close, he could smell Chris' shampoo. The brush of his baby-fine hair against Landon's cheek was just a tad damp. He'd showered before coming. God damn, that was sexy. It was hell pulling away from Chris and forcing himself to go back to his side of the table.   "What if I don't drink beer?" Chris asked, his thumb drawing up the condensation beading on the outside of the bottle.

There was that slight possibility that Chris was right. If he was, then Landon's instincts were way off base and that would surprise him. Landon prided himself on knowing just what others thought and did. "Then I'll drink it and we get you something that you'd like."

Chris chuckled, his eyes lowered demurely to watch as the water pooled beneath the bottle. "Beer's preferred, actually. And I especially like craft beer."

Landon gave Chris a genuine smile. "I know."

With a disbelieving snort, Chris lifted the bottle to his mouth. He swiped at the rim before tilting it to take a sip. Landon watched in rapt fascination as his throat bobbed to swallow. It was taking his willpower to keep his ass in his chair and not push Chris's bottle away to take those beer-slick lips in a hungry kiss.

Not appropriate behavior. At least right now.

He shifted in his chair to keep his jeans from choking at his rapidly stiffening dick.

"Thanks for the dinner invite. This first week at work has been killer," Chris said when he lowered the bottle. "Yelp says this is a decent place to eat."

"One of the best in the city. I went to college with the owner." Landon leaned back in his chair. Catching Chris's gaze, he held it as he drank from his beer. There was a flash in Chris's eyes, a tightening that caused these cute crinkles when his gaze stayed riveted on Landon's lips. He knew he had Chris's full attention. "And there's nothing bad on the menu."

Chris nodded slowly and picked up the menu. His eyes widened slightly before looking up. "Um...it's a little pricey."

"But worth it," Landon said. He slid the menu to the edge of the table.

That move didn't go unnoticed. Chris gestured with his menu. "Already know what you want?"

"I have my favorites and it's a matter of choosing what I want this time."

Chris focused on the menu again, flipping through the selection several times before he apparently settled on something. He added his menu to the pile. "I guess you must make pretty good money to afford eating here regularly."

The Omega was fishing for information. It was almost like a game for Landon to keep deflecting Chris's attempts, just to see how far the Omega would pursue it. Landon smiled, his shoulder lifted in a light shrug. "I come here a lot and have some favorites."

The waiter came not long after Chris set his menu aside. Chris got the chicken puttanesca with artichokes. Of course the Omega would order one of Landon's favorites. It made perfect sense to Landon. He settled on the gnocchi sorrentina, having a particular taste for basil and mozzarella. And a refill on their drinks.

Once they got their fresh beers, Landon leaned to brace his elbows on the table. "So I was able to coax you out for a dinner. Thanks for coming, by the way. You had me worried that you would say no."

"Yes, because I'm sure you're unaccustomed to the word."

Landon blinked rapidly but the small curve of Chris's lip clued him in that the Omega was having a go at him. This was promising. He was still facing the stone wall that Chris had erected between them but that one small enticing smile gave Landon a peek over the top of it. "I think you might be pleasantly surprised at how often I hear no. Not that I take it as the first answer. Never take no as the first answer."

"So you're a salesman?"

"If by salesman, you mean selling my charming personality in getting no turned to a yes, then I guess that's a fair assessment."

Chris laughed and he set the empty bottle aside to start the fresh one. "I am amazed at how you are able to openly deflect any attempt to get to know you better."

Landon grinned. Chris talking was a very good sign. It was when Chris grew silent that was frustrating. "Just like you're equally adept at keeping your wall in the perfect position so I can't get past it."

Chris leaned back in his chair and stared at Landon across the table. "I guess we all have our protective camouflage."

"I can still see you, though." Landon mirrored the way Chris sat. Leaning in was too aggressive and it put Chris instantly on edge. He definitely didn't want the Omega on edge.

"And what do you see?" Chris's chin lifted in defiance. "Since you're so perceptive and all."

Landon tapped his thumb against his bottom lip as he regarded Chris. The Omega's arms weren't folded across his chest, but they were rigid as he let his hands rest on the table top. He kept his face tilted down to peer out at Landon beneath his light brown bangs that fell artfully over his eyes.

Yet his breathing rate was more rapid than normal for a resting state.

"I see a young, ambitious Omega who wants to prove to the world that he can do just fine on his own," Landon started slowly. "He's probably at his first full-time position, although he worked hard during the internships he fought for and won by being hungrier for them than his competitors. So he has a leg up in his chosen field."

After a pause, making sure he held Chris's attention by taking another long drink from his beer, Landon continued. "He's fit and in shape, which means he doesn't spend his spare time behind the computer or sitting on the sofa eating crap food. New position, new to the city means he's continued to be frugal with his money, habits built from his time in college. He likes to do things for recreation that aren't expensive or require a lot of cash outlay to enjoy. But he's not about to turn down the opportunity to try something new in the city, either. He knows how to take any situation and turn it into an adventure."

Judging by the flush of color in Chris's cheeks, Landon knew he'd gotten most of that right.

What could he say? Just because he lusted after the Omega didn't mean he was only interested in the man as a quick lay. Otherwise, why would he have bothered to listen at all during their lunch the other day? Simply being in Chris's presence was alluring and enticing. His advance and retreat behind the wall he kept erected was more and more attractive to Landon. Chris was not one to give up anything without a fight.

"He's someone who wants to trust but knows the danger involved in trusting the wrong person. Yet there's still a part eager to reach out for that connection that makes his heart pound faster and his temperature rise." Now that got a reaction that Landon was hoping to see. The slight parting of Chris's lips in a silent gasp and the widening of his pupils.

Landon leaned in and dropped his voice to a low purr. "And someone who, despite his best intentions to keep me at arm's length with all his nos, wants to say yes when I invite him to dinner again."

The spell Landon wove almost worked. It was broken by something Chris's gaze darted to look at behind him.

A wall of expensive cologne hit Landon and he wrinkled his nose. It was instantly familiar. He remembered it from earlier that afternoon. He wasn't ready for the voice that followed it, standing just off his shoulder. "Some people are so predictable," a voice interrupted.

Instantly, the voice grated on Landon and his hackles rose protectively. He swallowed the growl that threatened to roll out of his mouth. Every muscle in his body went stiff. His fingers curled into fists as he sat back, his spine now rigid.

With a deep, centering breath, Landon twisted in his chair to look up at Clint Knowles's smug grin.

Well, fuck.

Chapter 9 - Chris

It made sense that Landon would know other regulars at the restaurant if he was a regular himself. Chris watched as the new Alpha approached the table. He stood, one hand tucked in the pocket of his slacks, the other resting atop the button of his suit jacket.

They were similar in many ways. Both Landon and this new Alpha were poised and confident. They both commanded the space around them. Their scents, both uniquely Alpha and lion, were strong to the point of making Chris light-headed.

Similar but with their differences.

Where the new Alpha had hair dark as midnight, with equally dark eyes that sparkled with mischief, Landon was his opposite with his golden eyes and honey blond hair.

The new Alpha was dressed in his obviously tailored suit. That wasn't one bought off the rack. Chris may not own a suit like that yet, but he knew one when he saw it. Many sleepless nights, he crawled the internet to look at all the things money could buy once he had enough he could afford them.

65

The biggest expense were the designer suits. Chris had very few things he lusted after. A perfectly tailored suit was one of them.

Watches were another and the one the Alpha sported on his wrist glittered in the ambient lighting of the restaurant. Rolex was Chris's guess. It was simple and tasteful.

This Alpha obviously stood out in the gastropub, but it didn't appear to bother him or make him uncomfortable.

Juxtaposed against the new Alpha was Landon's extremely dressed-down choice of clothing for the evening: Jeans and a simple button-down shirt. Boots and a plain, if functional, watch.

Between the two, this new Alpha was really the sort of man Chris wanted in his life. Someone who knew what he wanted in life and obviously went for it. The fruits of his labor were obvious.

"What can I do for you, Knowles?" Landon's voice had that soft roll of a warning growl that made the hair on Chris's neck stand up.

"Not a thing, except introduce me to your new friend."

Chris's gaze darted to Landon's face. His teeth were clenched, even though he was trying to be polite. It was obvious from the tension that made Landon sit rigidly in the chair there was no love lost between the two.

"Chris, this is Clint," Landon said curtly.

Clint stepped forward and extended a hand. Chris stood to shake it. Clint's handshake was just like Jeremy had coached him to do. Firm, confident, not too hard or limp. Held for just the right amount of time. Perfectly executed.

Clint Knowles as a smooth operator.

"Pleasure, Chris."

Chris smiled and gave Clint a nod before sitting down again. He was going to ask if Clint wanted to have a seat when Landon interrupted.

"There," Landon said, his voice taking on a dangerous tone. "Introduced. Don't let us keep you from wherever you were going."

"Even if I had pressing plans, I'd still make the time to rescue your friend from making a *drastic* mistake later."

What did that mean? Did Clint actually mean to disparage Landon's intentions like that?

Judging by the look on Landon's face, Chris guessed the answer was yes and it didn't make Landon happy at all.

Chris was new to the city, but he wasn't new to tense social situations. The tension ramped up to eleven and it was choking as the two Alphas stood off.

"Funny guy," Landon bit off. "Unless you consider the chicken a drastic mistake."

"Well, certainly not here, I'll grant you. I'm partial to their Bucatini all'Amatriciana. I do hope you chose the right wine, Landon. You were always a little weak in your tastes."

"If by weak you mean pretentious. We're both enjoying the summer ale, actually. Fresh batch."

"Ah. Beer. I'll grant you, a good choice, if a little pedestrian. Their brew is the envy of the area."

"It's a good thing you're not staying long enough to be insulted by its presence at *my* table."

Landon hadn't stood or given off any signals that he was willing to butt heads with Clint. Judging by the way Clint stood just off to

Landon's right, but not once looking at Landon when he spoke, definitely indicated there was a power grab in play. It was awkward to sit there as the two had their Alpha standoff.

What bothered Chris, though, was Clint's unwillingness to acknowledge that he had been invited to leave, however implicitly it was said. It was as if he was deliberately standing there to piss Landon off.

Chris himself felt torn down the middle.

On the one hand, only looking at Clint, he was all the things Chris wanted in his life. He was definitely attractive, and his Alpha scent mingled with his very expensive cologne.

There was something off-putting about his attitude toward Landon. Not just the air of superiority. Alphas always had that bold, confident, sometimes cocky, attitude.

He was actually being rude, but it was done so subtly that many wouldn't have noticed.

Chris noticed because it was a little bit of a turnoff. It was definitely more than just Alphas bumping chests. There was some deep resentment between the two men and Clint was definitely trying to provoke something with Landon.

69

After a long moment of tense silence, Clint's smugness melted away and he produced a card, extending it to Chris. "It was a pleasure to meet you, Chris. Perhaps we can talk another time when you're not otherwise engaged."

Now *this* was awkward. If he didn't take the card, he was being rude. If he did, it could be misinterpreted by Landon. Chris hesitated before he took the card and tucked it in his back pocket. He would try to explain why if Landon pressed him on it. "Thank you. It was nice to meet you, Clint."

Clint nodded politely and drifted away from their table.

It took a few seconds for his cologne to finally fade away.

Landon sat there, his brow furrowed as he stared off across the restaurant, most likely watching Clint leave. Chris thought it best if he didn't turn around, focusing on his beer.

Landon's silence was a little unnerving.

The tension broke a little when the waiter brought their food. After a moment, Landon rolled his shoulders and appeared to shake off the encounter.

Judging from the stormy look in Landon's eyes, Chris didn't think he would get off that easy.

Chapter 10 - Landon

Landon had to wait until he could no longer smell Clint's cologne before he risked speaking. By that time, their dinner had come and it felt like he'd let too much time pass.

With the way Chris was looking at him, he felt he owed the man some sort of explanation.

At least Chris hadn't gotten up and walked out.

He finally put his silverware to the side and took a long drink from his beer. "Chris, I'm sorry about that."

Chris glanced up, paused between bites. "It's okay."

"No. No, it isn't. I didn't handle that as well as I would have liked. It's left a bad impression on you and I'm sorry." Landon passed a hand over his face.

"I kind of got the impression you two don't get on very well."

Landon sighed. "You are right. I've known Clint for a long time. We grew up in the same neighborhood and went to the same school. Even went to college together. For as long as I can remember, he's just had this thing where he had to prove he was better than I was."

"I figured it was Alpha rivalry or something."

"It isn't really that. I'm not...I'm not *normally* bothered by him. He wants to compete over everything and I refuse to engage him. I figured if he saw that I wasn't going to play his game that he would eventually give up." Landon combed his fingers through his hair. His appetite was gone. The desire to move, to run and be out in the wild pulsed strongly through his body. "Instead, he doubled down on trying to drag me into his dick waving contest."

Chris fell silent and Landon was on the verge of calling it a night. His mood was dark and he feared that he didn't make a good impression on the Omega. Finally, Chris raised his hand for the waiter, who came over. "To-go boxes, please."

Landon's head snapped up and he looked quizzically at Chris. A shy smile spread across Chris's face. "I think we need to get out of here. You didn't look like you were going to finish eating and I'm not going to finish all this so why not get it to go and find something else to do for the rest of the night?"

That was not what Landon expected to hear but he wasn't going to turn down this gift. Chris was generous in his attempt to salvage the rest of the night. Meaning...Chris wanted there to be more to the night than just dinner.

At least it was Landon's hope.

Landon settled the bill while Chris loaded up the to-go cartons. They stopped by where Landon had parked to store the food.

Chris shoved his hands in his pockets. "So what's next?"

"We're not far from a park. They have roasted almonds if you're into that."

"I can eat my weight in them."

A great thing to hear. Landon chuckled softly, already feeling lighter now that they were out of the restaurant. City air wasn't exactly *fresh* air, but it was better than the closed off feeling of being trapped in the restaurant with all the people pressed around him. "Then come on."

They strolled along the sidewalk in the direction of the park. "So tell me who you are, Chris," Landon said. "Talk to me, let me hear your story."

Chris tilted his head to look at Landon from beneath his bangs. That was so unfair. It was a look, with just the right shadow across Chris's large beautiful eyes, to throw some mystery into the mix. "It's pretty boring. My dad was a deadbeat and my mom couldn't shake her drug habit, so I entered the system when I was about ten or so."

Landon walked with Chris, matching his pace and stride to keep their stroll to an ambling speed. Chris crossed his arms over his chest, hands rubbing over his biceps. There was a bit of a chill in the air, not that it bothered Landon. He liked it cooler. He liked to feel the chill on his skin.

He shrugged out of his jacket and draped it over Chris's shoulders to help warm him up. "Man, I'm sorry to hear that." It was a rough way to live a childhood.

"I was one of the lucky ones. Jeremy and Colin Robertson were married but Colin couldn't have kids of his own so they opened their homes to the foster system. I was placed with them." Chris glanced up into the night sky.

Landon looked up as well, to see what Chris was looking at. "You stayed with them?"

"Yeah. They already had four other Omegas they'd taken in. I went from being an only child, and neglected to boot, to living in a huge house with other boys."

"Wow. I can't imagine. I was an only child."

Chris's arm brushed against his as he swayed slightly into Landon as they walked. At first, Landon thought it was just one of those awkward moments of running into each other while walking and talking. Chris glanced up at him and grinned, doing it again to let Landon know it was on purpose.

Landon returned the smile and careened gently into Chris, knocking him slightly off balance.

"It was a bit of a culture shock. Since each of the brothers in my new family were from a different shifter species, there was some friendly competition on who got to ride shotgun when one of our foster fathers took us somewhere. Or who ended up having to do the dishes. Jeremy and Colin were amazing fathers. Took five misfit kids out of a system where the odds of being forgotten were almost one hundred percent, and gave them stability and safety. I vowed that I would take what they taught me and be self-reliant and self-sufficient. I guess that's why

I'm so driven to make sure this job works, you know?" Chris shook his head to clear the hair from his eyes. "I was independent when I was a kid, and even though I had these amazing role models who loved me, I want to get out on my own as quickly as possible. It's important that I create my own success, and that whoever I end up partnering with understands and respects that."

"That's really inspiring." When they got to the park, Landon guided them along one of the smaller pathways. It was late enough at night that there were very few joggers out. The lightposts cast puddles of yellow light along the path as they walked. The city traffic grew muted against the silence of park until it was a dull background roar.

"What about you?"

Landon glanced at Chris. "What about me?"

"Oh no, you don't get out of telling me something about yourself."

He laughed. "Fair enough. Like I said, I'm an only child. Raised by the same parents all my life. One of my fathers owned a business and it was sort of taken for granted that I'd take over the business. Not exactly what I wanted to do. I tried to get out of it by getting a degree that *wasn't* in business." Landon shoved his hands into his pockets and watched the path in front of them.

"But you did take it over?" Chris asked.

"Sort of." Landon gave Chris a mischievous grin when the Omega glared at him. "Mostly, I learned how to hire good people to run the business for me. They know more about it than I do so I just sign the checks and give my vote of confidence when they need it." He nudged at Chris, sending the man slightly off the path. "One of the best managers I have at the company is a bonded Omega. He has bailed my company and my personal ass out of the fire so many times that I think he's due for another raise. So you know, I get it that you have a desire for a career that is your own. That you're not defined by your partner."

It took a few steps before Landon realized Chris had stopped walking. Chris was standing in the middle of the pathway, looking at Landon with this odd expression on his face. Had he said something wrong? Landon risked walking back to Chris, coming to a stop in front of him. "Chris? Was it something I said?" Landon didn't usually make big missteps like that, but Chris managed to keep Landon just enough off balance to make him question himself.

Chris still said nothing, his teeth pulling on his bottom lip as if he were thinking about something. Landon waited patiently. Whatever was on Chris's mind, it was enough to give the Omega pause.

With no warning, Chris grabbed a handful of Landon's shirt and dragged him forward. Landon reached out to hold Chris by his hips, partly to keep his balance and stay on his feet with the heavy tug. Unexpectedly, their mouths collided, warm lips pressed against his in a surprised, but very welcome, kiss.

Not how Landon imagined the night would go.

Chapter 11 - Chris

At first, Chris thought he'd made a huge miscalculation. Landon stiffened when Chris clumsily pressed their lips together. Just as quickly, though, Landon's arms wound around his waist. Landon's body heat warmed Chris in the cool air of the night. The leather jacket slipped off his shoulders as he wrapped his arms around Landon's shoulders. He lifted to his toes to press for more.

His lips opened and Landon's tongue swept in, deepening the kiss even further. It morphed from surprised to claiming within the span of a few breaths. Landon's body was hard as it pressed against Chris. The Alpha was built like a solid brick wall. If the man worked out, it showed. If he didn't, he was doing something right because Chris was enveloped in Landon's embrace and it was as if the outside world was no longer there.

There was no way real life would slither in with the way Landon, through a simple kiss, managed to possess Chris with breathtaking authority.

Chris wanted to submit to him. The desire tugged deeply at his gut. To feel the press of

Landon's rapidly hardening erection pressing against his abdomen was a startling realization. It shouldn't be surprising, but after what happened in the restaurant, Chris wasn't sure how things would go the rest of the night.

One kiss inflamed need in Chris like he'd never experienced before. He wanted to crawl up Landon's body and wrap his legs around the man's waist, demanding to be taken. What had started as an innocent expression was quickly ramping into something far more needy.

With effort, Chris pulled away. He dropped to flat feet again, licking at his swollen lips. His face heated in embarrassment when he realized just how turned on he was. That he was willing to cast all of his standards aside to feel Landon covering him, possessing him.

Landon blew out a soft breath. "That was…"

"Sorry," Chris said quietly. "I don't…"

"Don't be. Don't be sorry. I've wanted to do that since I first laid eyes on you, Chris."

Chris laughed. "Why didn't you?" After all, the attraction between them was obvious and had been from the time Landon pressed against his back in the coffee line. If Landon had pressed the issue, Chris would have been powerless beneath that level of passion.

"Because I wanted to get to know you," Landon said with a small grin. "I mean, you're hot, but...I like listening to you talk. Kissing you would have interrupted that."

Chris looked down and took Landon's hands in his, twining their fingers together. "It would have been a nice interruption."

"I don't doubt that, but I kind of like you being a bold Omega." Landon closed his fingers around Chris's. He pulled Chris forward and urged him to wrap his arms around Landon's waist. He was wrapped in Landon's arms again and the cool of the evening air was quickly supplanted by the heat of their bodies as they pressed together.

"Bold or pushy?" Chris leaned in to Landon, clasping his hands at the small of Landon's back.

"Same thing."

"Then why don't you take me home."

"I like the cut of your jib, mister. You're lucky we don't have far to go," Landon said. He leaned in to whisper against Chris's mouth. "Unless we're going to your place."

"Yours." Chris wanted to feel Landon filling his ass, and his place had to be closer than Chris's. He wasn't willing to wait any longer than necessary.

Landon ducked down for another kiss. This time, it wasn't a surprise. It was a promise that Chris wanted to collect on.

***

Chris squirmed in the front seat of Landon's Land Rover. That should have been the first indication that Landon wasn't quite as broke as he first suspected. How does a nearly homeless guy afford a vehicle like this?

When Landon pulled up in front of one of the newly restored historic apartment building complexes and parked the truck, Chris stared out the window before he registered that Landon had even turned it off.

"You coming or are you going to sit out here all night?" Landon asked as he climbed out.

Chris scrambled out behind him and shut the door. He looked up at the building.

This was not what Chris was expecting to see. He was, in fact, expecting to pull up in front of some run-down tenant building. One where he'd have to make sure he didn't go barefoot for fear of getting something.

Landon led him into the building, their hands clasped tightly together as the Alpha pulled Chris along.

In the elevator, all the walls were brass panels, polished to a high shine. Soft muzak played in the background as Landon punched the top floor button.

Top floor? A *top floor* apartment? Chris blinked a few times to let that sink in.

Landon was full of surprises tonight. He may be closer to Chris's ideal Alpha than he originally assumed.

Not a smooth move to make assumptions like that.

There was no time for Chris to feel bad about misjudging Landon, or feeling a little like a social climber. Landon backed him in the corner, crowded him against the wall of the elevator. Cupping Chris's face, Landon kissed him again. He slid his thigh between Chris's legs to press against his half-hard-and-getting-harder cock. It was a filthy promise of a night that Chris wouldn't soon forget.

He was okay with that. Landon was all Alpha. Pure allure and testosterone. His kiss was the final seal on Chris's need and he whined softly against Landon's mouth. His fingers closed around Landon's shirt as he dragged at the Alpha impatiently. Landon growled in reply, the sound striking every chord in Chris like a well-played instrument. His cock twitched fully erect in his slacks and he rocked his hips against Landon's thigh as it lifted between his legs. If he could have Landon filling his ass *now*, Chris would drop his jeans and bend over.

The elevator slowed to a stop. Just before the ding, Landon pulled away, his tongue swiping at Chris's lips. "I can't wait to get you into bed."

"Then get your keys out and get me in your apartment."

"Yes, *sir*," Landon drawled.

The door dinged open and Landon led Chris down the short, elegantly decorated hall. Any other time, Chris would have appreciated the cost of the art on the walls alone, but right at that moment one thing was on his mind.

Landon's cock. Landon's tongue. Landon's bed.

The moment the door slammed shut, Landon had Chris pinned again. He liked how the bulk of the larger man pressed him against the door. Their mouths clashed again, and Landon's kiss claimed him like Chris had only dreamed an Alpha could.

Instinct took over and Chris's body was willing to submit without another word. It was a dizzying sensation to need someone so intensely that all reason fell by the wayside in a laughable heap of abandoned resistance. There was no resistance with Landon. The way Landon manhandled him away from the door to start the shuffle-dance down the hall to the bedroom left Chris weak in the knees.

The journey from the front door to the bedroom was a blur. The moment the front door shut and locked, Landon was on Chris again. Gone were the tempered and even kisses. Chris couldn't get out of his clothes fast enough to suit him and Landon was still far too overdressed by the time they collapsed on Landon's bed.

With Landon's body weight pressing him into the mattress, Chris found he was softly purring. It felt perfect to have Landon covering him like that. Landon's cock was a hard line poking at his stomach. "Hey," Landon said with a cheeky smile.

Chris shook his head and lunged up for another kiss, desperate to breathe in Landon's presence. When he finally tore his mouth away to take a breath, Chris was panting. A small keening rose in his throat. "Landon, stop being a jerk."

Landon's laugh echoed in the room as he pushed off of Chris, sliding down the bed. Roughly, he parted Chris's thighs. "Take it easy, Chris. I want something first." Now even with Chris's cock, a wet spot on his stomach, Landon licked with a soft wet tongue up the length of Chris's shaft.

Right at the tip, Landon formed a soft 'o' to suck at Chris's head. Chris was already so sensitive and needy that he surged up, his fingers burying in the beautiful mane of honey blond hair. "Landon!" he squawked out in surprise.

Landon smiled, looking up at him, and slowly sunk down over Chris, sucking him in completely. He planted a hand in the middle of Chris's chest and forced him to stretch out.

Still holding to Landon's hair, Chris balled up his other fist in the covers on the bed to hang on as Landon wasted no time in blowing him. Chris's eyes squeezed shut as he was dragged along for the ride of an amazing blow job. "Please don't tease me, Landon," Chris begged.

The soft hum that started in the back of Landon's throat vibrated straight up Chris's cock into his groin and he arched in impatience. He panted from need. "I need your dick in my ass, you bastard."

Landon lifted his mouth off Chris's cock. "Then give me what I want, Chris." He sucked a finger in his mouth to coat it and pushed into Chris's ass. Mouth back on his cock, Chris twisted from the double assault. A gentle curve of Landon's finger and that perfect spot caused sparks to fill Chris's vision as he came hard, bucking beneath Landon's weight until he was done. Totally done and spent.

With a final suck, Landon kissed the inside of Chris's thigh softly before he crawled back up to brace on hands and knees over Chris. His hair fell in a curtain around Chris. With a sated smile, Chris traced Landon's red, slightly swollen lips with his thumb. "Holy shit, I hope you don't expect me to do anything else."

"I do, actually." Landon lowered to take Chris's mouth in a long, deep kiss. He could taste himself on Landon's tongue. It instantly spiked in him and his lust for the Alpha began to build again.

"I need a minute," Chris panted against Landon's mouth.

"That's all you'll get."

Landon rolled off Chris and he whined at the loss of body warmth and Landon's comforting weight. The Alpha didn't stay gone long before he was back with condoms and lube.

Chris laughed weakly. He shoved at the lube. "Don't need that," he said. "I'm so wet for you I'm gushing a swimming pool."

"I could tell but I just wanted to make sure."

With an exhausted sigh, Chris pushed to gain distance between them so he could roll onto his stomach. Landon gave him room to lift to his knees but he left his shoulders and head pressed to the bed. That was all the strength he had.

Landon kept a steady hand at the center of Chris's back as his cock found home and started to slide into the Omega's body. "My God, Chris. Your ass is so hungry for my cock. Just sucking me in."

When their hips met, Chris sighed again, this time as contentment washed over him. It was so natural to feel Landon buried in him. *Finally* buried in him.

The comfort of Landon's weight returned, braced over his back as the cadence of thrusts picked up. Chris closed his eyes and fell into that deep space within that allowed himself to enjoy what Landon's mere presence was doing to him. It was a spiraling, heady feeling of comfort. Of belonging. Of satisfaction in the most intimate way. Almost as if, crazy thought, that his body was made specifically for Landon.

The hot puffs of breath against his shoulder as Landon thrust, making growling and purring noises as he pumped, not only brought a smile to Chris's lips but his cock began to stir again until it bounced with every connection of their body.

He was able to lift to his hands and brace, steady now to push back against Landon with every snap of the Alpha's hips.

"That's it," Landon said in a sex-rough voice. "Work with me." The Alpha smoothed a hand down Chris's arm and lifted it, guiding his hand to his own stiff cock. "Bring yourself off, Chris. I tasted you before; let me feel you now."

Just as he was asked, Chris picked up a stroke that kept pace as Landon pistoned into him. Landon's fingers curled around his hips to drag Chris back. The thrusts grew shorter, faster, and from listening to Landon's breath, he could tell the man was close. Chris kept time with him.

"Chris." Landon's growled warning was strained.

He liked the way his name sounded as Landon clearly held back.

A few more strokes and he came again, hot stripes that spilled across his fingers, the bedspread, hitting the forearm that fought to keep Chris up.

Landon tossed his head back, Chris's name a shout that echoed around the room. He bucked beneath Landon while the Alpha hung on, riding his own climax.

Finally, Chris's arm gave out and he face-planted on the bed. Landon doubled over Chris's back, his sweaty forehead pressed against Chris's spine, hot breath puffing with each exhale.

He couldn't stay on his knees any more. Chris reached back to pat at Landon's thigh. The Alpha tipped them to the side. Spooned from the back, Chris basked in afterglow, wrapped in Landon's protective embrace. Chris allowed himself to consider what he'd just done. Casual sex romps weren't his thing. Getting caught up in the moment perhaps wasn't his finest moment.

He still had his career to think about. A new job. Trying to get his own life together. Landon certainly delivered in bed, no doubt about it. The Alpha was a complication he couldn't afford, no matter how surprisingly enticing he turned out to be.

Chris resolved to allow himself this one moment of weakness. It probably shouldn't happen again.

No...it wouldn't happen again.

It *couldn't* happen again.

Chapter 12 - Landon

Landon watched the sun come up through the blinds of his bedroom. Drifting in and out of sleep, he finally gave up getting any real rest. That wasn't a complaint. He had trouble remembering the last time he had so thoroughly enjoyed a night with someone.

Spending the night before with Chris drove a lot of points home for Landon.

Sex with just any Omega body wasn't what he wanted in his life any longer. He wanted something that offered more stability.

Stretched out next to the sexy, sweaty and sated Chris sat comfortably with him. It was *nice*. Landon didn't want to chase Chris out of his apartment. He didn't want to try to escape into the early morning before he was missed.

What he wanted was what he had right at that moment.

Contentment.

Chris tucked against him, their legs tangled together and his breath a soft tickle against the skin of Landon's chest, it really couldn't get much better than that, could it? He didn't see how it was possible.

The impulse to roll Chris over and wake him with another round of sex was cut short when the alarm on his phone chimed softly. Always a light sleeper, Landon didn't need anything obnoxious to wake him. Annoyed that he hadn't turned the damn thing off anyway, the irritation gave way to resignation when he realized the alarm was also to remind him of the board meeting.

Damn, he hated those things. All they did was talk about what they needed the meeting to talk about, and then talk about it some more. Maybe some planning to meet again to talk at a later time. Meetings, in his opinion, were a waste of time. They were also a necessary evil. He had implicitly promised Carolyn he'd be there. Putting in an appearance was required.

He was loathe to disturb Chris, though. In fact, it was preferred that he stay in bed like this all day. Having Chris in his arms in the morning was as natural as breathing.

However, the damn alarm was just loud enough to cause Chris to stir. With a cute smack of his lips, Chris rolled away and freed Landon's arm. With no reason to stay in bed,

Landon carefully rolled out and went to start the coffee. He checked his emails while it brewed and sent a reassuring text to Caroline that he would *really honest and for true* be there for her stupid-ass meeting.

Landon fixed Chris's coffee like he had ordered from the cart the first day he saw the Omega and set both of them on the side table. He crawled back over to the sprawled form and nuzzled at the back of Chris's neck.

It took Chris a few moments to register Landon's presence and he arched into the affectionate kisses. He purred happily and cracked one eye. "What time is it?" he murmured against the pillow.

"About 5 a.m. I hate to wake you, but I want to make sure you get home in time to get to work." That was the downside to this. Rolling out of bed because of work. The next dinner invitation would be on a Friday night to ward off such complications like work and responsibility.

Chris made a small noise in the back of his throat. It was so cute Landon had to nip at the back of Chris's shoulder. "I made coffee, if that makes things better."

"Marginally." Chris rolled over, crowding against Landon until he'd thrown an arm and leg limply over Landon's body.

He liked that Chris was a cuddler. "This makes it hard to drink the coffee."

"In a minute," Chris said over another yawn. "You're warm."

"Nor is this getting you ready to take you home."

"*Waa~arm*," came the singsong reply.

Landon chuckled softly and let his eyes drift shut. He was careful not to get too comfortable or they'd both be late for work. He remained still until the heat of their bodies soon made them sweaty, and in that not very pleasant sort of way.

With a huff, Chris stretched and sat up. "Last time I go on a date on a weeknight."

"Funny, just what I was thinking."

Chris glanced over his shoulder to give Landon a smile. It penetrated straight through Landon to land squarely in his stomach. There, it broke apart into a hundred butterflies that beat their wings wildly. It was the kind of smile that Landon loved to see.

Open. Trusting.

A smile he didn't see often enough out of anyone. A smile that was lacking in his life.

"Ugh, I hate the thought of getting back into dirty clothes," Chris said with a wrinkle of his nose. "And without a shower."

"Doesn't have to happen." Landon rolled to sit on the side of the bed. He handed Chris his coffee, who took it gratefully and sipped at it. "Grab a shower here. I have some spare sweats and a shirt that can get you home and you can get dressed for work."

Chris' eyes were closed and there was a look of bliss on his face.

Orgasms and coffee. Two guaranteed things to bring out that beautiful expression. Landon made a note of that for future reference.

As far as he was concerned, there would be a future instance for that future reference.

With a nod, Chris enjoyed his coffee in silence as Landon dug out the clothing.

It was unfortunate that they were under a time limit. Landon would toss all that aside and pin Chris down for morning sex. Not going to happen.

That didn't stop him from a hand job in the shower when he was able to pin Chris against the shower wall and coax yet one more orgasm from the Omega, complete with the same delicious whining and begging he got the night before. As perfunctory as it had to be, Landon wanted to have that one image seared into his brain if he was expected to sit through a boring ass meeting all day.

Taking Chris home on his bike was faster than the Land Rover. Not to mention more selfish. Who was he kidding? Landon loved how Chris held on to him, his arms wrapped around tightly as they zipped through the early morning traffic.

He pulled up outside Chris's apartment, killed the engine and stripped off the helmet. Chris, not used to it, had trouble getting the strap on his and Landon took that opportunity to draw the Omega close while he did it for him.

Chris held the helmet and looked at it, as if he were searching for something before handing it to Landon. "Thanks for dinner last night and the loaner clothes." He held his hands out to his side.

He actually looked ridiculous, in that completely adorable way, in clothes that were a few sizes too big. With his mussed hair and large brown eyes, Landon's heart clenched in his chest. He hadn't driven off and already he missed Chris.

Cupping Chris's chin, Landon pulled him in for a chaste kiss. It would be too easy to deepen it with the hunger that rose inside him. That wasn't helped by the way Chris leaned in when their mouths met.

"I should get inside," Chris said as he pulled back. Instead of stepping away, he leaned in for another kiss.

"Probably. If you don't want to be late." Landon chased Chris's mouth to keep the connection between their lips.

"Mmm," Chris hummed happily for the final kiss before he planted a hand in the middle of Landon's chest and pushed firmly. "I need to stop that."

"It *is* addicting."

With a laugh, Chris stepped back, gaining more distance. "Maybe. I'll um…call later in the week to arrange getting these clothes back to you."

"There's no rush. Have a good day at work."

Chris nodded. He fumbled with his keys. "You too."

Landon waited until Chris disappeared into the building before he jammed the helmet back on his head and kicked the bike to life.

Landon didn't want to go. After Chris...he knew what that meant.

He didn't want any other Omega. The one Omega Landon wanted was upstairs getting ready for work and frustratingly out of reach for him.

Leaving was making his heart hurt.

That was not acceptable.

Chapter 13 - Chris

If it was possible to float up the stairs to his apartment, Chris definitely would have. After that last kiss goodbye, his feet didn't touch the ground. His head was filled with clouds and floating thoughts of pure bliss.

Once in the apartment, he dialed his brother and waited for Max to pick up.

The sleepy "'lo—" drove home the fact it was dead early in the morning and his brother wasn't even awake. The brief stab of guilt fell beneath his good mood.

"Morning, sleepyhead," Chris chirped cheerfully in the phone.

"I hate you." Max cleared his throat. In the background, he heard something fall to the floor. A brief profanity-filled grumble and Max was back again. "Why are you calling me at godawful o'clock?"

"Well," Chris began casually, "I wanted to tell you about my date last night but if you're going to be such a grump about it, it can wait for when I come home next month. Talk to you lat—"

"You bitch," Max interrupted. "If you hang up now, I'll come over there and pound all your cereal into dust. Dish."

Chris laughed softly. "It was good. *Really* good. I'm glad I went."

"He didn't wimp out and take you some place cheap to eat, did he?"

"Oh hell no. We went to Piazza Navona for dinner."

"No shit. I hear they have great beer."

"They do. You should go."

"When I can sell a kidney, maybe." The cracking of Max's jaw when he yawned was audible over the phone. "Did you two hit it off?"

Chris flopped onto the sofa to stretch out. He pulled the hoodie Landon let him borrow for the ride home and inhaled. It had two scents that made Chris's senses come alive. Whatever fabric softener Landon used, Chris need to get some for himself. It was heavenly.

Beneath that, deeper tones. The scent of an Alpha. An extremely attractive, slightly maddening Alpha.

"I can hear you sighing," Max said with an amused tone. "So I'll take that as a yes."

"I don't know if you could say 'hit it off' is exactly it." Chris let his head fall back. "I mean, he's still really cagey when I try to get to know him better. He finds ways to deflect my questions."

"Could be that you're a nosy little shit. Did you ever consider that?"

Chris laughed. "I know I am, Max."

"And you have a tendency to be closed off as well. Especially when meeting new people."

That one hit close to home. Closer than he was comfortable with. "I'm working on it."

"No need to be defensive, bro." The sounds of Max making coffee filled the silence as Chris fought the desire to tell Max he wasn't being defensive.

Which meant he was being defensive. "I don't have this trouble at work. I talk to everyone and we all get along fine."

"Of course you do. You're not trying to get laid by *them*."

That was hard to argue against. "I guess not."

"You *did* get laid last night, am I right? Please tell me that you didn't let this perfect opportunity go to waste."

"There is more to getting to know someone than having sex with them, Max," Chris said primly. His face heated from the memory of just how close he did 'getting to know' Landon.

"You did, you little minx," Max crowed in victory. "Did he blow your mind?"

"I am not going to have this conversation with my brother." Chris glanced at his watch and lurched to his feet. "And I have to get ready for work."

"Killjoy. Are you at home now?"

"Yeah, Landon dropped me off a few minutes ago."

"*Landon*—"

"Shut up, Max."

"Next time, take an overnight."

"Good God. I'll talk to you later. Sorry for waking you."

"It's all good, Chris. I'm glad you are home safe and that you got biblical with *Landon*. You needed it. You were getting so uptight you squeaked when you walked."

"I'll talk to you later," Chris repeated and killed the call.

Since he'd already had a shower, he only needed to tame his hair and get dressed. Too bad casual day wasn't an unofficial policy for the firm or he'd wear Landon's sweats. Seemed a shame to have to change but he couldn't go dressed like this.

With great reluctance, he took them off and folded them reverently, leaving them at the foot of his bed. When he got home that night, he'd put them on again.

For as long as he could get away with it, he'd wear them. At least until those scents faded.

The kiss before Landon zoomed away on his bike was going to linger in his mind for some time to come.

Yes, the sex was amazing, and if Chris could have his way, they'd do that a lot more often.

The kiss was the topper to his morning. Filled with unspoken promises that Chris secretly hoped that Landon would keep.

Promises that would have Chris purring for Landon in a heartbeat, eager and willing to submit to the Alpha. Moving heaven and earth to please Landon and allowing the man to care for Chris like he believed Landon would.

It was unspoken but the great affection Landon felt for him was palpable in the air in that one simple good morning kiss. Was it love?

If this was a Disney movie, maybe. The deep romantic Chris managed to keep subdued surfaced with the thought that it was. Even though he barely knew the man, Chris knew he didn't believe he was in any danger of being hurt. Worry and fear were the farthest things from his mind.

Driving to work was an exercise in focus if he didn't want to cause a pileup on the interstate. With the way Chris's mind continued to blank out, shutting out everything around him except his night, and morning, with Landon, it was a miracle that Chris got to his desk unscathed.

He did manage to make it without killing anyone.

Now at work, the real challenge began. With mindless work ahead of him getting ready for a presentation, his thoughts continued their happy reflection on the past twenty-four hours.

"Hey, Chris." Clarissa perched on the corner of his desk and picked up his paperclip magnet to play with the metal clips.

"Hey." He looked at her warily. She was grinning from ear to ear. "What?"

"You're just really far away. Being a big sister, I think I recognize that look."

Chris couldn't stop the blush that burned his skin. He was positive he was red all the way down to the tops of his feet.

She burst out laughing. "Oh my God, I was just joking! I had no idea until just now."

"Whatever," he grumbled. With a mulish look, he crumpled up one of the pages he had to be recycled and threw it at her. She shielded it easily, catching it.

It just made her laugh harder. "How close are you done to having the presentation done? I am trying to finalize the agenda and need to know how much time it's going to take."

"You could have called or emailed." The heat from Chris's skin started to fade, and with a determined focus, he looked at the screen and realized the last half hour's work was gibberish.

"I know, but sometimes I just have to stretch my legs."

With a shake of his head, Chris blinked his eyes hard. If he was going to get through his work day, he needed to focus more on work and less on Landon. "I'm just about done. Should take twenty minutes to present."

Clarissa slid to her feet and smoothed down her blouse. "Will you be ready for being number two in the order?"

Chris nodded, furiously deleting the trash words. "What time is the meeting again?"

"In ten minutes."

"Shit!"

"Stop thinking about whoever it is and get to work," she said with a sly wink. "You'll need to make about ten copies and don't forget to upload it to the shared folder."

"Right, right," Chris grumbled. He waved as she headed off, and with grim determination, focused on the last of his presentation. He pulled his wallet out and gave it a toss on his desk. The card he got last night from that rude Alpha slid out. He picked it up to look at it.

Clint Knowles, CEO Venandi Technology.

He interned briefly with them when he was in college. He didn't ever remember seeing Clint there.

Whatever. The guy was rude as hell. He tossed it down and turned to focus on the presentation.

He spent enough time daydreaming about Landon. Now was the time to work. This presentation would justify their taking a chance on hiring them.

He finished with minutes to spare. He sent the print job to the printer and uploaded to the shared folder Clarissa opened for the meeting, grabbed his wallet and rushed to his first official company meeting and presentation.

This was a chance to prove his worth to the company.

He couldn't afford to screw this up.

Chapter 14 - Landon

Landon snarled in frustration. Fumble fingers were having a hell of a time trying to tie his damn tie. He hated these things. It was like a noose around his neck. A collar and leash. Yes, he did pay a hell of a lot of money to have his suits specifically tailored to fit him. His shirts were custom. He spent money on his clothing. Not because he had the money to spend, but because if he was going to be crammed into a damn suit, it was going to be comfortable.

Still. He turned to regard his reflection in the mirror. Clint Knowles could take a long walk off a short pier. He wasn't the only Alpha in the city that looked good in a suit. Landon knew he cut a nice figure in the suit. He wore it like a second skin, regardless of how he hated the damn thing.

Of course, the suit meant he had to take a car into work instead of his bike. That was a shame.

It was only one day out of how many he could get away with not showing up in a suit at all? Conduct most of his business through his VPs, over the phone and via emails? He'd suffer through important meetings like this in the suit if it meant he was free the rest of the time.

All he had to do was get through the day.

***

Caroline greeted him at the elevator, handing off an iPad and touching at it to wake it up. He stared at it for a moment, then glanced at her.

"Welcome to the twenty-first century, Mr. Williams. If you remember, last year we started to streamline to reduce paper waste."

Landon touched at icons to pull up the business agenda. "When's lunch?"

She whacked him on the shoulder. "You're insufferable. All the other VPs are here so we can get started as soon as you sit down. If everything goes well, we can wrap everything up by lunch."

"What's the big thing on the table today?"

For that, she teased out a folder and handed it to him. "Venandi Tech. We think they're getting ready to make a big move. Alan has discovered some telltale signs that Knowles has spies here feeding him information. We're keeping a low profile about it until we get more information."

He tucked it under his arm as he followed her into the conference room. "Let's get this over with."

An hour into the meeting, Landon was bored stiff. Before they covered the big items on the agenda, a whole host of little crap had to be attended to. Business housekeeping. Stuff that couldn't hold Landon's attention if it had been stapled to his forehead.

Projections and new market avenues, more reports, test cases, big news in the tech industry that could affect them; Landon had a hell of a time keeping his yawning to a minimum.

While his head of accounting gave her report for quarterly earnings, figures Landon had already seen in his weekly FaceTime meeting with her, he pulled his phone and pulled up Chris's contact. He was at least *trying* to be discreet, but if it drew anyone's attention, they'd have to get over it. He was the CEO.

How's the morning going?

He tapped at the volume so the alarm wasn't obnoxious. Resting it on his thigh, he would feel it vibrate when he got a response.

After a few moments, it did.

Ugh. Project meeting, You?

Same

You have meetings? ;p

Landon covered his mouth so no one saw him chuckle.

Cheeky

Accounting wrapped up their segment and they took a ten-minute break. Landon pushed back in his chair so he didn't have to hide the phone as he thumbed in a reply.

Interested in going out to dinner again?

James, his head of IT, sat next to him and they discussed some options to upgrade current security and a rewrite of their section in the employee handbook to handle IP rights for work done at the company or while on company time. The phone vibrated in his hand. It was hell waiting for their discussion to end before he checked it. But he was the boss and he did need to put in some employee time if he wanted the company to continue operating smoothly.

Sure.

Landon's chest expanded in delight. So he hadn't imagined things with Chris. The Omega was maddeningly difficult to read at the best of times and equally difficult to draw out into any sort of engaged discussion, but once Chris opened up, Landon found himself more and more drawn under Chris's spell. Chris was the first Omega that Landon had actually wanted to see *again*. That rarely happened. None of the other Omegas he'd gone out with were all that interesting to him.

So Chris agreeing to go out to dinner again made getting into the suit and suffering through boring discussions worth it.

The meeting kicked in again and Caroline gave her presentation in conjunction with James. From what Landon gleaned of the discussion, they feared they were losing proprietary information in a leak that was directly tied to Venandi Technologies.

Conversation was lively around the table as they discussed their options. Landon took that opportunity to Google restaurants. He trusted his head of HR to do what was necessary to root out the problem.

"...investigation of new hires brought in for the past six months."

The table grew quiet and Landon suddenly felt like all eyes were on him. He glanced up, acting like he was lost in thought over what she had said. Truthfully, he only caught that last bit. Gaging the look on the faces of his other VPs, Landon straightened in his chair and made a show of 'thinking about it more'. After a long silence, he nodded. "If that's the best way to close the leak, then that's a good start."

That was apparently the right answer and Caroline smiled. "Thank you, Mr. Williams."

Now…about those restaurants…

Chapter 15 - Chris

The rest of the week was a blur for Chris. After the text from Landon asking him out for dinner, they had exchanged a few more texts to settle on a time on Saturday.

The anticipation was a little heady. An Alpha was interested in him. Interested enough to ask him out on a second date. And not just any Alpha, but Landon, who kicked up the butterflies in his stomach just by looking at Chris.

On the heels of that, his manager decided that Chris had the hang of his projects and decided to cut him loose on a few to head up on his own.

All in all, not a bad first month on his own in the city.

He called Jeremy and Colin to give them the excited news. At least about the project. He wasn't quite ready to say anything about Landon, although he was positive Max, with his big mouth, had spilled the beans.

"It's just small things, nothing company changing or anything," he said as he twisted back and forth in his chair. It was Friday and the vibe around the office was high, with everyone just riding the clock until it was time to go home.

"Don't sell yourself short. You kill it, and you get bigger projects," Jeremy said.

"Your star is rising, Chris!" Colin shouted from the background.

He wouldn't go that far, but it did feel pretty good to be given even this small amount of responsibility.

"So are you coming home this weekend?" Colin's voice was a little closer to the phone now.

"Doesn't look like I'll be home any time soon," Chris said apologetically. "I have plans this weekend and next is the wedding of a buddy of mine from college."

"And the weekend after that, Colin has an out-of-town engagement," Jeremy said with a sigh.

"It's okay, Chris," Colin said. "You have your own life now. Come home when you can, okay?"

"I will, Colin. I promise."

From three cubicles over, Buzz waved and pointed to his watch. Chris silently nodded. "Okay, I have to run. Love and miss you guys."

"You, too, Chris," Jeremy said.

"Call again soon," Colin shouted again.

With a smile, Chris hung up and headed for the small grouping standing at a desk. Buzz was shutting down his workstation. "Hey, Chris. A few of us were going out for drinks at Blink's. Want to come?"

"Yes, please. After this week? Let me grab my jacket."

Powering down his own computer and grabbing his briefcase and jacket, Chris felt pretty good about his life. He was making friends, he was starting to date, he was settling into his new job.

A sense of contentment spread over him. Things were coming together for his life.

***

"They have a great selection of appetizers." Russell flopped onto the bench and scooted to the middle.

Blink's was jam-packed for a Friday night, but they were able to score a circular back booth so they wouldn't have to stand around the bar.

Buzz introduced him to other Omegas in the office on his third day there — Russell and Dixon — and they had banded together. Most days, they had lunch together in the cafeteria. Other than Buzz, who had been there a year, the rest were relatively new hires like him. He was the newest, only there a handful of weeks. The rest had been there for months.

They all had gone out of their way to make Chris feel right at home.

"Make room for Sarah. She said she was going to be late."

Chris pulled the menu over to look at the appetizers. "Who's Sarah?"

"From HR. You probably saw her all of five minutes when you got your company ID taken."

A younger woman joined them at the table. The moment Chris saw her, he did remember her from his first day. Buzz introduced her before she sat her drink on the table. She flopped onto the bench next to Buzz, forcing all of them to shift over to make room. "Nice to see you again, Chris. Please tell me I'm in time to start the party?"

"We just got our drinks," Buzz said.

"Good!" she said brightly. She reached around Buzz to grab a menu.

"I thought you were going to be late," Buzz said.

"I was, but Caroline took pity on me for all the long hours I pulled this week."

"She was looking pretty harried when I saw her earlier this week," Chris said. "Not that I know her or anything, but she seemed...rushed."

Sarah took a large gulp of her drink. "They have some project they're implementing in looking at new hires. The higher-ups are pretty mum on it so don't ask for details. But it's got us all jumping."

Dixon visibly slumped. "For someone in HR, you are sadly lacking in the gossip department."

She licked at her finger after she swirled it in his glass. "Not completely. Rumor has it the CEO has been putting in more appearances at the office."

Russell leaned in. "No way."

Sarah folded the napkin around the bottom of her drink. "Yes way. I saw him in the halls in the executive suites upstairs several times. I'm sure it's him."

Chris listened in rapt attention. He had heard the CEO was notoriously hands-off of the company, and had not seen the man yet.

"I hear he's been sick," Dixon said, "and that's why he stays away."

Sarah smirked at Dixon. "If you really mean 'ridiculously good-looking' as a metaphor for sick."

Chris laughed. "He's good-looking?"

"Saying he's good-looking is like saying the Statue of Liberty is kind of tall." Buzz pulled his phone and thumbed through it. "They had a picture of him on the old website before they revamped it."

Chris leaned over to watch as he pulled LeoTech's website.

Sarah waved a hand over his phone. "Don't bother looking. They pulled them down when they revamped the website. Then Rennie went out on maternity leave and they won't let her temp touch the website until she's back. But trust me, the guy is drop-dead gorgeous."

"There's not an Omega at the company who doesn't dream about him," Buzz said.

Sarah nodded in agreement. "Some of us nonshifters, too."

"Did he ever get bonded?" Dixon asked.

Russell shrugged. "I didn't know he was looking for a mate."

Buzz shook his head. "I think it's a lucky guy—"

Sarah elbowed him. "Hey—"

"—or woman who can nail his foot to the floor."

"You know he has a mate. All the good ones are taken." Sarah sighed dreamily. "What about you, Chris? Are you seeing someone?"

"Sort of? I think?"

Sarah threw her hands up in mock surrender. "Figures. I give up. I'm going home. Someone pay my tab."

Dixon took a sip of Sarah's drink. "You should if you're going to drink that swill."

Chris was disappointed when Buzz wasn't able to find a picture of the CEO. "It'd be nice to know what he looks like in case I ever run into him in the halls," Chris said, taking a sip of his beer.

"Oh hello." Buzz put his phone down on the table and picked up his glass. "Speak of the devil and he will appear."

Everyone at the table craned to look in the direction Buzz was staring.

"Oh my God." Russell grabbed Chris's sleeve and tugged hard. "He's here?"

Dixon craned his neck to look. "Where? Is he alone?"

"God, you're such an opportunist," Buzz said. He nodded his head in the direction of the bar and leaned in to Chris. "That's him, with the long hair."

Chris searched through the strangers until he saw who Buzz was talking about.

Even though the man had his back to them, there was no mistaking the long, familiarly blond hair. His heart leaped in his throat. What were the chances that there was another man in the city with that same kind of long hair and solid build that filled out the jeans and t-shirt in such a way as to send Chris's pulse racing?

When the man turned, there was absolutely no mistaking him.

Landon.

Russell finally broke the spell at the table. "Damn, he's gorgeous."

"He could dominate me any day of the week," Dixon added.

Sarah rested her chin in her hand. "He could have the pick of anyone in here and they'd willingly follow him."

Chris clutched at his shirt. His chest constricted and it was hard to breathe. Landon was the CEO of LeoTech?

He was Chris's *boss*?

Was this what Landon was hiding? It didn't make sense to keep something like this...to *lie* about something like this. Chris's head was light and he blinked against the spots forming behind his eyes. He needed to get out, get some air. "I need...get up please."

Dixon grabbed Chris's arm. "Chris, you don't look so good."

"I don't...I mean...I need a minute." Chris motioned for Dixon to let him out of the booth.

He grabbed his jacket and briefcase. "I have to go," he said, and his voice sounded so far away. He was afraid he'd pass out right there.

Panic gave way to anger and the blood pounded in his ears. Everyone at the table was talking, looking at him with concern. Any other time, he would have appreciated it. At the moment, he needed to get some distance.

"I'll see you guys Monday," Chris said in a hurry as he swiveled on his heel.

His path to the door took him right by Landon. The Alpha's eyebrows lifted when he recognized Chris. He was surprised to see Chris there.

Chris knew the feeling. His anger won over his surprise and panic. With clenched teeth, he glared at Landon as he pushed out of the pub.

Behind him, he heard his name.

Landon called out to him. Tough. Chris didn't need to talk to him right now.

Didn't *want* to talk to him.

He pulled his phone from his pocket to call for a ride. He needed distance.

Chapter 16 - Landon

This was not how Landon anticipated his Friday night would start. Chris's expression looked like it could melt through steel. There was no time to find out what the problem was before Chris pushed out of the pub. Whatever the problem was, Landon's instincts told him he did not need to let Chris get away from him without talking.

Whatever the problem was, he knew he needed to figure it out and, if possible, make it right.

He sat his drink on the bar and followed Chris, who had stopped once outside, swiping angrily at his phone. "Chris!" he said loudly to get the Omega's attention.

Landon jogged to where Chris stood and touched his elbow.

Angrily, Chris jerked his arm out of Landon's hand. He glared up at Landon. Whatever he'd done, it had pissed Chris off really badly.

"Hey," Landon said. "I wasn't expecting to see you until tomorrow night."

Chris crossed his arms and gave Landon a really good impression of a bitch face. "I'm sure you weren't."

Uh, okay. Landon wasn't sure what this was about, and it looked like Chris was going to make him work for this. He took a cleansing breath to start again. "I'm not sure what's going on, Chris. Care to fill me in on what I've done?"

"Have you done anything?" Chris asked tartly.

"That's what I'm asking."

"I can tell you what you *haven't* done. You haven't come by my desk to welcome me to *your* company. I thought all CEOs gave welcome speeches or something."

Landon scrubbed at his face. Already a headache was forming behind his eyes. "Right. I guess you figured it out."

"Oh." Chris stuck his chin out stubbornly. "I was supposed to figure it out? Like it was a test? How did I do?"

"For fuck's sake. What the hell. Of course it wasn't a test."

"Then I'm sure there's a *very* good reason why I was left in the dark to feel like a complete ass thinking you were someone else." Chris's arms crossed defensively over his chest. "Why you kept acting like you were no one important."

"In the grand scheme, Chris, I'm not—"

"Only the CEO of one of the top tech firms in the state." For all of Chris's anger, his voice was steady but his eyes flashed. Landon took a steadying breath. Now was not the time to be turned on in the face of his wrath. It was powerful, though, the intensity rolling off Chris in thick waves. And arousing. He wanted to pull Chris into his arms and kiss his anger away.

Landon pulled his keys out. "Let's take a ride and talk about this."

Chris watched people walk into the pub. "I don't know; standing out here and talking about it suits me just fine."

"Chris...what can I say to make this right?"

"Well, we can start with why you lied to me."

"I didn't."

The withering look was cute if Chris weren't so serious. "Seriously, you're going to go there."

Landon spread his hands. "I didn't lie. I just...didn't tell you the whole story."

"Oh, well that makes everything better."

"Jesus. Chris, what do you want from me? You're seriously pissed because I didn't feel like I needed to announce to you who I was? 'Hi, my name is Landon Williams and I'm the devastatingly handsome CEO of the company you've just started working for. Want to make out?'"

Chris dropped his arms and leaned forward. "It would have been a good start. No," he said, speaking through clenched jaws, "you didn't *technically* lie. You just failed to tell me the whole story. Please. A lie of omission is a lie. You. Lied."

The pools in Chris's eyes cut Landon to the bone. He watched Chris struggle with keeping his emotions under wraps. In the face of the accusation, the *truth*, Landon's resolve melted away. He believed his reasons were valid at the time.

Now, standing here with the first Omega Landon had been really interested in getting to know better in a long time, he was watching that slip away from him. He breathed out slowly. "You're right."

Chris stepped back, blinking rapidly. He scrubbed at his eyes. "What?"

"You're right. It was a lie of omission. I did lie by not fessing up to who I am. My reason seemed good at the time but now...I guess I didn't really have a good reason. I wanted you to like me for me, this me. Who I am here," and Landon placed his hand on his heart. "Not for the money or the company or...anything."

He thought Chris had softened a bit while he explained himself. Until the wall slammed down again.

"So you didn't trust me to make that determination on my own?" Chris's jaw clenched again. "Didn't think I'd rise to the occasion by making that decision myself?"

"It's not that I didn't trust you—"

"You have dodged every direct question since I met you, Landon. I tried to let it go, get around it. Figured you were just hard to get to know." Chris waved his arms before letting them fall limply to his sides.

"You haven't been exactly all that open either," Landon shot back. He got that he had fucked that part of it up, but he was getting a little tired of being painted as the only uncommunicative one.

"Oh, so now your lying to me is *my* fault?"

"That's not what I said."

Chris threw his hands up.

Landon risked stepping forward and placing his hands on Chris's shoulders. "Chris. Please, can we take a ride? I think we need to talk this out somewhere more privately." It was risky, and for a moment, Landon didn't think Chris would agree.

After a moment of deliberation, Chris nodded. "Fine."

Landon led Chris to where he parked.

"Where are we going?"

The Land Rover roared to life. "A place I don't think you've discovered yet. It's a shifter park here in the city. Shifters can run there in their animal form in freedom."

Chris buckled in and sat back with his arms crossed over his chest. "It's been a while since I've shifted. Before college."

The anger had bled a little out of Chris's voice. Landon would take that as a small victory.

The rest of the drive was made in silence. Landon didn't want to risk destroying that small gain he'd made by getting Chris in the Rover.

He parked and motioned for the Omega to follow him to a small blind off in the wooded area.

Stripping off his leather jacket, Landon didn't wait for Chris before he started his transformation. The process was quick, and when he dropped to his hands and knees, he was already in his lion form. He continued to watch Chris, shaking his mane out to its full magnificence.

He caught the slight widening of Chris's eyes when he was in full lion. Lifting his nose to the air, he could smell the scent of Chris's arousal. His expression was still annoyed but the tightening around his eyes was starting to soften.

Chris dropped his defensive posture and started the shift himself. When he was finished, Landon huffed out a soft breath. Even as an Omega, Chris's leonine form was just as attractive as his human. His mane wasn't as full as an Alpha's, and his lion form, smaller than an Alpha, was still larger than a female's.

Chris extended his front paws and pushed back, taking a deep stretch before he shook his shorter mane out. With a haughty turn, Chris's tail bapped Landon on the nose as he strolled away to flop down in the shade of a large bush.

Desire for Chris stirred deep within his body.

It was obvious Chris was still annoyed at him. He wasn't making it clear whether he'd fight or submit to Landon.

It was hard to get a read on just how badly he screwed up. Landon suspected it was pretty bad.

Chapter 17 - Chris

At first, Chris fought the disorientation of going from two legs to four paws. It had been far too long since he had indulged the wild side of his nature. He sniffed at the wind and closed his eyes to let the wash of scents roll over him. The smell of the city, a food vendor at the entrance to the park, fresh asphalt from some road project, the green of the woods.

Mostly, the scent of an aroused Alpha close to him. His eyes blinked open sleepily as he lolled onto his back, paws in the air. Landon in his lion form was truly a sight to behold. Alpha in its purest form. His blood sang through his body, his instincts pressed against the front of his mind.

He wanted Landon so much it was sinful. He wanted to swipe at his nose and pounce on him in an invitation to run, to chase, to fly through the woods and be a part of his nature that he ignored in his pursuit of finding his own way in life.

Chris was still angry with Landon. If he were feeling generous, and he certainly was *not*, Landon wasn't wrong in saying that he outright lied. He hadn't. At no point did Landon ever tell him a falsehood. Neither did he actually *answer* any of Chris's direct questions.

Which made Chris angry at himself because the signs were there. They were *right there* in every evasive answer Landon swung his way. He chose to ignore them because the closer he drew to the illusive Alpha, the more Chris was intrigued. Every moment with Landon had Chris falling further under his spell.

Omitting the truth felt like a betrayal. It was a blow to his trust that Landon didn't believe that Chris knowing who he was would have changed things.

Even if it held an element of the truth, much to Chris's consternation. He *had* judged Landon when they first met. He *had* made assumptions that turned out to be false. And he *had* almost walked away from Landon due to who he believed Landon was. At least until he fell in love.

Regardless, it stung that Landon hadn't trusted him.

A shift on the wind drew Chris's attention back to Landon.

Lust turned to frustration as Landon paced back and forth in front of him. Good. Let him be frustrated. Let him work for this. Chris was due that at the very least.

Landon stopped and released a throaty growl. It vibrated through Chris's body, touched him in the deepest parts of his soul. Rising to his paws, Chris walked up to Landon, regarding those amazing honey-colored eyes before reaching out and swiping a heavy paw at Landon's nose.

With that challenge, Chris took off at a run through the woods.

He didn't immediately hear the sounds of pursuit, as if Landon had to process what had just happened before moving in pursuit. Behind him, Landon's roar echoed through the park. That spurred Chris on to run faster to evade him.

The sounds of four paws as Chris raced on drew closer behind him. Landon's breath as he ran to catch up helped Chris gauge how far behind the Alpha was. Something caught his back foot and lifted, pulling Chris off balance. He landed wrong and tumbled nose over tail, twigs and leaves kicked up in his path until he slid to a stop.

As he scrambled to his feet, Landon was almost on top of him. Chris didn't have time to get

138

another head start so he turned to face the Alpha. Once Landon was within reach, Chris took another swipe at him. No claws, just the heavy weight of a paw against Landon's muzzle.

Landon ducked and shook it off as he pressed closer, trading one blow for another as Chris backed away and Landon circled around.

His desire was to fully submit to Landon. Chris couldn't. Not yet. His anger still smoldered beneath the surface. Landon still had to prove himself.

Following him out of the pub was a good start. Attempting to apologize, another good move. Bringing Chris out to the park and his anger was starting to diminish as he gave himself over to his lion nature to operate on instinct. His instinct told him Landon was sincere.

That didn't mean he was going to make it easy for Landon. No, he had one more thing to prove.

Was he Alpha enough for Chris to finally submit fully to him?

It was key and Landon appeared to understand this. He was stronger than Chris and could have easily taken him down violently.

How Landon handled it would be the proof on what to expect from the Alpha.

They tussled and traded blows, claws retracted except for the few times Landon extended them to tangle in Chris's mane to drag him down. It didn't hurt Chris. In fact, it amped his excitement higher.

Landon hooked his claws in again and instead of pulling as Chris expected, he *pushed* and it took Chris off balance. He landed heavily on his side. Landon's hold in his mane pulled the Alpha on top of him and there, Landon was able to pin Chris.

Chris looked up into those heavenly golden eyes. Yes. He wanted this Alpha. It was clear this Alpha wanted him. Enough that he was willing to do what it took to have Chris.

The rest of the wall finally crumbled to dust and he relaxed beneath Landon and shifted back to his human form. With a tilt of his head, Chris bared his neck, offering it, and his heart, in submission to Landon.

He hoped Landon would take care with it.

Chapter 18 - Landon

A low growl wound out of Landon as Chris shifted back to his human form. Chris challenged him and pushed at him and it aroused the Alpha in him like he hadn't experienced in a long time. The intensity struck a deep chord within. His thoughts revolved around Chris every waking moment. The desire to be in the man's presence was a constant companion, especially when Chris was out of reach.

Now, here was this delicious Omega who had won his heart by simply existing and he was offering himself to Landon in a way that spoke to the primal part of his nature. It hooked into his soul and drew him further into the spell Chris cast on him. It touched off fantasies of having Chris submit to him in the wild. Fantasies that had fueled the past week.

With his nose, he nuzzled at the bond site, that spot at the juncture of neck and shoulder. With his rough tongue, he licked at it. It wrung a shudder from Chris, followed by a low moan. Reactions Landon would have from Chris again and again if he had his way.

Landon shifted back into human as well, lowering himself to cover Chris' body with his own. He felt the Omega's arousal, mirroring his own. Warmth pressed against him, a different sensation from the cool of the evening that pressed against his back.

Chris stroked along Landon's arms and played with his hair until it fell around them in a golden curtain. It gave the illusion of privacy, although Landon was certain that no one would happen upon them. At this time of night in the park, strolling around was not on any shifter's mind. He was certain no one would interrupt.

"Chris," he said softly, following it by an equally soft kiss. "Want you."

Chris chased his mouth, taking more teasing kisses. He lifted his thigh to press against Landon's dick and Landon inhaled sharply. "So do I. So I'm not sure why you're waiting."

Sex outdoors had its issues, but at that moment, Landon didn't care about roots or sticks poking his knees. What he cared about was feeling Chris's body stretched around his cock as they roared each other's names to the night sky. "Are you wet for me?" Landon purred.

"I think you talk too much." Chris closed his fingers around Landon's shirt and lifted, dragging it off his body in one motion. Landon lifted so it cleared his torso before going to work on Chris's slacks.

"You'll have to have these cleaned," Landon said.

"I'll send you the bill."

With a possessive growl, Landon ripped at the button and zipper to get them down so he could access Chris's body with nothing in the way. A brief, vocal protest died away when Landon ducked to suck Chris's cock with one motion. He drew all the way down his shaft until his nose brushed at the brown hair at the base. Chris arched up with a cry, his hands beating down on Landon's shoulders. "OhGod—"

Yeah, Landon liked when Chris's voice broke like that. He sucked with enthusiasm until Chris was begging, chanting Landon's name over and over.

"Landon," Chris choked out. "Please. I need to feel you."

With a slurpy pop, Landon sat back on his heels to urge Chris to turn over. They worked Chris's slacks down over his hips to present to Landon. The heady scent of Chris's arousal hit him like a tidal wave. His heat was thick and it triggered every instinct in Landon. He slid his fingers along Chris's ass, dragging the slick along with it as he pushed it into Chris's hungry hole.

Chris released a keening cry, his head dropping to rest on folded arms while Landon finger fucked him. His cock was screaming in his jeans to be released and find the blessed warmth of Chris's ass. Landon pushed the feeling down, allowing it to simmer in his groin until he was satisfied Chris was on the verge of going insane.

The continued nonverbal vocalizations rose and fell from Chris as he wiggled and shifted beneath Landon. Chris finally hit the breaking point when his head snapped up and he looked over his shoulder with a frustrated invitation buried in his hard glare. He rocked back hard against Landon, almost pushing them both off balance. "Landon—" he growled out.

With a smirk, Landon pulled his finger and shifted to his knees. The twigs and rocks were nothing more than a minor irritant. The sweet torture of waiting until Chris was so needy he relied on his lion instincts to drive him.

He sighed when his cock slowly slid into Chris. Comfort settled over him like a warm blanket. Chris drove back hard until their bodies touched and Landon gasped at the sudden sensation that swamped his senses. It stripped away the last veneer of control he had as he pounded into Chris. He rode Chris hard, thrusts punishing as he slid into the tight channel.

Everything around them dissolved into a mist. Landon's focus was on Chris and him alone. The sound of their breath, the touch of their skin. He braced over Chris, resting against the Omega's back as he pushed into him. He stroked along Chris's cock. The sounds of their coupling filled his ears.

Chris's body jerked when he came, bucking beneath Landon and drawing him back to the present. His cock throbbed as he released and coated the ground. The sweet constriction around his own shaft brought stars to Landon's eyes.

He slowed his pace as Chris caught his breath, fingers digging furrows in the forest floor. "Shit, Landon," he breathed out heavily.

Landon grinned and nipped playfully at the back of Chris's shoulder. He took his time sliding in and out of Chris, giving the Omega a moment to catch his breath.

Chris bucked against him, a clear sign he wanted Landon to move again. He was more than willing to oblige.

Now able to focus, Landon gripped Chris's hips tightly to hold him still. He released his hold on his instincts, allowing his body to respond as it needed to find his own release. Chris was his.

Chris would always be his. No one would take the Omega away from him.

Out in the wild, under the trees and the stars, Landon covered one of Chris's hands, curling so their fingers were tangled together. He pressed his face against Chris's neck, short breaths coming faster as he moved. Chris tilted his head to nuzzle and Landon was positive he heard Chris purring.

The sound short-circuited Landon and his climax washed over him like a tsunami, swamping his senses as he rode the bliss of sweet release until his body was liquid. Landon filled Chris's ass, his own mind blissfully empty except the cloud of hormones that floated them both along as Landon tipped to take them both to stretch out on their sides.

The night started out shaky.

It ended with one of Landon's biggest fantasies. Chris in the wild, with him.

No pressures, no angst. Nothing between them.

And no more lies.

Chapter 19 - Chris

Chris was feeling very good, thank you very much. After having been thoroughly fucked at the park, he and Landon managed to wobble their way to the Land Rover and get to Landon's apartment. He dangled a bottle of beer from his fingers, barely holding on to it and recognizing the danger that he could drift off at any moment. Fall asleep, bottle slip to the floor…and a waste of good beer as well as a mess to clean up.

He shifted on the couch and tried to get less comfortable. Not as easy as it sounded. Landon must have paid a fortune for the oversized behemoth. It was like the Cadillac of sofa boats or something. Every time he was still, he sunk into the comfortable cushions and lulled him into a sense of contentment.

"Your couch is from hell," he called from the living room. Partly to make sure Landon didn't forget him and partly to keep from falling asleep.

Landon turned from dinner preparations at the stove to lean over the breakfast nook that separated the kitchen from the expansive living space. "Sucks the energy right out of you, doesn't it?"

"Does it come in a less energy sucking version?" Chris fought to sit up and almost failed. He persevered and was able to get on his feet before succumbing to the lure of the couch. He padded in bare feet to the kitchen to get a fresh beer. His hair was still damp from the shower they both had to take once getting home.

Sex in the woods was romantic right up until the point they realized they were muddy.

Not that Chris was complaining. The way Landon looked at him when they were in the woods after the run? He would have had to be blind not to see the depth of emotion swimming behind those golden eyes. It sent a shiver down his spine thinking about it now.

Landon wrapped his hand around Chris's and drew the beer to his lips to take a sip. "You cold? Do I need to turn the air down?"

Chris batted Landon away and drew his beer protectively to his chest. "Get your own, beer thief. And no, I'm fine. I'm swimming in your sweats as it is."

"You know," Landon ducked into the fridge to get something. He closed the door with a bump of his hips and twisted the cap on his beer, "if this keeps up, all of my clothes are going to end up at your place."

"Then you'll have to come over to my place to spend the night and shower. That way, you can wear them back home again."

"Blackmail, then. Got it. Then grab the colander and rinse that head of lettuce." Landon gestured with a spatula. "Start tearing it for the salad."

Uncovering the lettuce on the counter, Chris pulled the colander from the dish rack and set it in the sink. "Now I have to work for dinner? Seems a bit unfair since it's your fault I didn't eat tonight."

Landon set the spatula aside and went to Chris, wrapping him from behind. "I'm sorry about that."

"Which part?" Chris was still a little peeved about how the whole thing went down.

"All of it. Not telling you. Upsetting you when you found out how you did. Making you miss dinner." Landon kissed the side of Chris's neck.

Tilting his head out of the way, Chris rallied to keep his annoyance in the present. That was hard to do when Landon was solid warmth against his back. The comfort of his arms promised to keep Chris nestled safely away from the cares of the world. "Make dinner worth it and I'll consider forgiveness."

Landon kissed his neck one more time before pulling away. "That was the plan."

Chris busied with the task of getting the salad ready while Landon stayed with their dinner.

"Landon," he asked after a few minutes of productive silence.

Landon covered the skillet and turned the heat down beneath it. He stretched across Chris to pull down two plates. "Yeah?"

"Can you tell me who you are now?"

"I'm Landon Williams, CEO of LeoTech. I took over the family business when my father had a stroke. It left him bedridden for years. In order to prevent the company from bankrupting, I stepped in. I didn't want to. I was content to work in R&D."

"So it was supposed to be temporary?"

"Yep." Landon patted Chris on the hip to shift to the side so he could get the silverware. "When my father decided to retire, it was left to me. I didn't want to let my folks down, you know? Being CEO wasn't really in my life plan. I'm not wild about all the day-to-day minutia of keeping the doors open. But it's not like I have a choice. Clint Knowles, you know the guy that came up to the table the first night we went together?"

Chris nodded that he did.

"He's had his eye on LeoTech ever since he first started up his own company. He's made several proposals for us to merge. But my dad built LeoTech from nothing. I wasn't going to give up his dream. So...I stayed on as CEO. Learned to delegate—"

"Perfected your pickup technique at coffee carts," Chris said with a laugh.

Landon spread his hands and grinned at Chris. "And the rest is history. It's all about familial responsibility. I take it seriously, even if I don't like what I'm doing. In time, I learned to delegate, which turns out to be what's best for the company *anyway*."

Chris's anger melted further. So his *omission* had nothing to do with being afraid of intimacy or anything like that. Only to protect his family's company while doing a job he didn't like. He couldn't imagine his life going that way. Chris knew what he wanted, moved at warp speed to get it and wouldn't let anything derail him.

Still floating on endorphins and the high of sex and having run in the wild after years of being stuck in human form, Chris wasn't sure how to communicate that he could forgive Landon without it sounding sappy. There was another way.

He hooked his hand over Landon's bicep and drew him away from the stove until he was backed up against the kitchen sink.

Landon stumbled along behind him and leaned heavily against the counter. Without preamble, Chris dropped to his knees between Landon's spread feet. He quickly worked Landon's sweats down his hips, exposing the half flaccid cock.

Encouraging Chris by cupping the back of his head, Landon sighed when Chris covered the head of his cock with his lips. Teasing licks at the rim and along the veiny shaft with a soft, wet tongue was enough to make Landon hard within moments. "Oh yeah," Landon said on a soft sigh. His fingers slipped through Chris's damp hair and pushed it from his eyes. "Keep your eyes open. I want to see them."

Chris grinned around Landon's cock and slipped over him in one motion. Landon was larger than he could take in and had to use his hand to make up the rest. Precome leaked from the head and Chris swallowed greedily. Even after a shower, Landon's Alpha musk was strong. It made Chris dizzy being so close.

He used one hand to help guide him as he slurped over Landon's dick, the other to hold to Landon's hip to keep him from moving around too much. With Landon's hand firmly held at the back of his head, Chris had enough leverage to pick up speed.

A purring growl resonated deep within Landon's chest.

It was the sound of contentment and Chris readily identified with it.

He stopped sucking and ducked further beneath to lick and suck at Landon's balls. Landon's grip tightened in his hair. Chris was worried he'd pull a handful out. "Jesus, Chris."

Chris pulled back and looked up the length of Landon's body. Landon's head was thrown back and his chest heaved. Watching carefully, Chris sucked one into his mouth to roll it over his tongue softly. A tremor shot through Landon like lightning. Oh, he liked that reaction. A lot.

"Thought you wanted to watch my eyes," Chris reminded him helpfully.

Landon's head dropped forward and looked at Chris with a heavy-lidded gaze. "Then why did you stop?"

With a soft chuckle, Chris kept his gaze locked with Landon as his mouth slowly slid back down the shaft. Landon released his death grip on Chris's hair. Now free to move, Chris stopped teasing Landon, working him up to bring him off.

It didn't take long for Chris to taste the precome and feel the hardening of his head to know Landon was close.

A thrilling shiver slithered down Chris's spine. He was hard in his sweatpants and his own cock twitched in anticipation. That could happen later. At the moment, Chris wanted to taste Landon when he finally cut loose, to watch as the Alpha tipped over the edge.

He wasn't disappointed. Landon gasped, his chest heaving with deep breaths as he approached his release. When it hit and the first splash of come hit his tongue, Landon groaned heavily. His eyes were glassy and unfocused but he kept his attention on Chris as the Omega eagerly swallowed him down.

Only when Landon was forced to stop Chris did he pull away. He wiped at his saliva-coated chin before resting his cheek against Landon's hip.

A feeling of contentment washed over Chris. Yeah, Landon shouldn't have left him in the dark. Knowing the circumstances behind how it all happened made it easier to forgive.

He smiled up at Landon. The Alpha stroked his fingers through Chris's hair. He didn't say it but a thank you was clear in his gaze.

That was enough for Chris. They could start from there and build forward.

Chapter 20 - Landon

If there was a way to make this night any more perfect, Landon was failing to figure out how. While arrogant to say, it was true that his dinner turned out amazing. Chris gave the most amazing blow job Landon had received in years. He had an evening of running through the woods and sex that blew the top off his head.

Couldn't get much better than that.

Now they were both drowsing on the couch, staring at the television. Some movie was on that sucked rocks. Network television always chopped the hell out of movies, butchering them beyond reason. But the remote had been moved at some point during the night and he couldn't be bothered to find it.

Chris was drifting in and out of contented sleep. One huge mass of relaxed, blissed-out Omega who had curled around him as they were slowly swallowed by the energy sucking couch.

Landon had half a dozen things he needed to do before he dragged Chris off to bed for a proper night's sleep.

Well, sex, then sleep.

With Chris's breathing growing deeper and deeper, Landon was reluctant to move the man off him to go do something as pedestrian as the dishes.

Honestly, he was comfortable. In more than the usual way of having had a filling dinner, some beer and a night that wound down to something intimate. It resembled contentment like Landon hasn't experienced before.

There was no rhyme or reason for how he felt about Chris after knowing him for such a short time. There was no doubt that Chris was his Omega.

His.

Where this took them next was anyone's guess but for the first time in his life, Landon knew that Chris was meant for him.

His phone buzzed on the coffee table as someone left him a text message. They learned early at the company that calling Landon wasn't a good idea. He hated talking on the phone. He would if it were necessary but if they took the time to prime him with a text first, things went much better for everyone concerned.

He had to stretch to reach it, careful that he didn't dislodge Chris.

It was a text from Caroline.

call me asap

He thumbed the call button and listened to it ring. Caroline picked up on the fourth. "Landon, I'm sorry for interrupting."

"Please tell me you're calling from Aspen or someplace far away from work. I will be terribly disappointed to know that my VPs don't take their weekends off when they can get them."

She gave a very unladylike snort. "That's next weekend, depending on how quickly we can get this resolved."

Landon frowned. "Get what resolved?"

"The new hire investigation?"

Landon pursed his lips. He felt like he should know what she was talking about, but it wasn't coming to him.

"Oh for the love of...the suspicion that Venandi Technologies has someone in our company? Corporate espionage? You were paying attention in the meeting last week, weren't you?"

"Of course I was," Landon lied. Chris turned, not even opening his eyes, and it freed Landon's arm. He eased off the couch and headed to the bedroom to talk so he wasn't disturbing the sleeping Omega. "So what do you know?"

"We have a few people on our radar, but right now the most likely person we're looking at is Chris Robertson."

Blood drained from Landon's face and he felt light-headed. "Alright." There had to be some mistake. "Are you sure?"

"We're still gathering information, but a couple of things stand out that point to Chris. He had interned with Venandi during his senior year in college. And we discovered one of Clint Knowles's business cards on Chris's desk. It was sitting out near his phone."

"What does it say on his resume?"

"Nothing outright. It was buried in the related experience bullet points."

"And the application?"

"Nothing was mentioned."

No. That wasn't possible. Not after tonight. Not after...any of this.

He scrubbed at his face and sat on the bed before his knees buckled out from under him. "What's the next move?"

"Well, it's all just circumstantial right now and it may go nowhere. We'll be interviewing him when he comes in first thing Monday morning."

Landon sucked in deep breaths, like he'd just been punched.

"Landon, you there?"

"Yeah. I'm here. Uh...do what you have to, Caroline. I appreciate your efforts and for calling."

"Sure. Have a good weekend, Landon."

"You, too." Landon killed the call and let the phone drop to the bed.

Chris was spying on LeoTech for Clint?

He didn't want to believe it. A deep part of him didn't think it was possible. It simply wasn't in Chris's nature. But things started stacking up too coincidentally. More than he was comfortable with.

His desire to believe that Chris was innocent warred with staring at some troubling information. His deep down belief that Chris was *his* versus Caroline's word. His HR VP wasn't a careless person. She was almost always positive she's right before she says anything.

His instincts still denied it, but his anger was gaining momentum.

Who was it that had bitched him out in front of the pub about lies of omission? Who was it that faced him down with anger about trust?

Landon went back into the living room. He sat on the coffee table across from the sleeping man. "Chris. Wake up. We need to talk."

Chris's eyes fluttered open. "I'm awake. I wasn't sleeping. Just drowsing." His sleepy smile cracked his heart and Landon almost caved, wanting to completely dismiss Caroline's suspicions as being wrong.

But too many other things piled up.

"Chris," Landon said. He hoped his voice sounded steady but it was taking everything he had to keep his anger under control. "Um...there's no way to really ask this except directly. Did you used to work for Venandi Techologies?"

Chris lifted to brace on one elbow. "I wouldn't call it work, exactly."

Landon lurched to his feet. He couldn't stop the snarl from escaping his lips. "And what *would* you call it, *exactly*?"

When Chris didn't immediately answer, Landon whirled around to see Chris blinking at him in surprise. "I um…well, I interned there for a summer. It was only three months."

"And you didn't think that might be important? To let me know that you worked for my *competition*?" Landon clenched his fists to stop the shaking.

"I…it never came up, Landon," Chris said. He swung his feet to the floor. Unsteadily, he rose and timidly approached Landon. "I included a mention of it on my resume. What's going on? You seem really angry."

"There is no *seem* here, Chris. I am angry." The words were out, hard and biting, and Landon did nothing to try to stop them. "You used to work for the competition and you fall into bed with me and I find out that you barely mention it when you applied to work here? Let me see," Landon posed as if he were thinking. "I believe that's called a lie of omission. And a lie of omission is a lie. Do I have that right?"

Chris went white as a sheet. "Landon, I…I didn't lie about this. I thought I made it clear when I

163

started working for LeoTech but honestly, the experience at Venandi wasn't all that helpful. It filled a hole in my resume."

Landon's blood pressure went through the roof. Blood rushed through his ears and his anger had fully taken root. "You gave me so much shit about my not divulging I was actually the CEO of LeoTech and now you have the balls to stand here in *my* apartment and tell me that your working for the competition, who is actively looking to bury me, that you didn't think it was all that important to mention it to me?"

"Landon, wait. I think we need to sit down—"

"No. *We* don't need to sit down. What *we* need to do is call you an Uber to take you home because you need to leave and I'm not in any mood to drive you anywhere."

Chris reached out, his fingers wrapping gently around Landon's forearm. He yanked his arm back. "Chris, you are close to crossing a line with me that won't end well for either of us."

"If you'd just let me explain—"

"Like you were willing to let me explain? Hypocrisy, thy name is Chris Robertson."

Pulling back like he'd been burned, Chris stepped back. Tears welled up in his eyes and he chewed on his bottom lip. "Landon, please—"

"No please. Just get out." Landon stormed from the living room. "You know the way."

Pacing the length of his bedroom, it was only a few minutes later he heard the front door click shut.

A deep part of him knew this was all some huge horrible mistake. It tried to convince Landon that he was making a very bad mistake.

The anger wouldn't shake loose, all-consuming in its rage as it stormed through his mind.

He was such an idiot.

Chapter 21 - Chris

It started with Chris feeling out of sorts.

Landon kicking him to the curb without allowing him to explain anything had been bad enough. The anxiety that came out of that was the hardest for Chris to get his hands around. While the bulk of it was Landon's reaction, the accusation itself was just as troubling. If Landon thought he were a corporate spy, then that obviously meant that management suspected it as well.

HR grilled him for the better part of that morning, Chris fighting the rising bile in his throat. He just wanted to throw up.

He hadn't been fired, which meant they didn't have enough information.

By then, the damage had been done.

Word spread quickly through his department. Shawn, to his credit, tried not to treat Chris any differently. It was obvious there was some doubt in his mind, anyway. Once the project Chris had been spearheading was wrapped up, no more project leads came his way.

The teams he had been assigned to treated him professionally. From a distance.

During staff meetings, there was this imaginary proscribed area around him. No one risked sitting too close to him.

Lunches were a solitary event.

Friday night out with his coworkers ground to a halt.

Chris went from fitting in to being left out. The distance and avoidance from people he was starting to call friends hurt him.

It wasn't personal, Dixon had told him when Chris was able to get him alone. They needed to protect themselves. Guilt by association and all that.

Chris understood, but it left him isolated from any support and it drove the loneliness home.

Through it all, his anxiety kept him so wound up that he fought down sick feelings every morning before going to work. The weekends were less filled with anxiety, but the sick feeling stayed with him.

He considered that he was coming down with something but running through the list of symptoms for cold or the flu or even food poisoning didn't fit. Something else was going on.

In the drug store to pick up more toothpaste, Chris passed by the section where the pregnancy kits were on sale. A small nudge in the back of his head spurred him to pick it up. It was a whim purchase.

Surely he wasn't pregnant, was he?

Thinking back to the night when he and Landon fought outside Blink's, he couldn't remember if Landon used a condom. He didn't remember it *specifically* at least. There was a chance, however.

Staring at the positive result on the stick proved it.

On top of everything else, as his world fell apart around his ears, he was pregnant.

Could his life get any worse than it was right now?

Chris sat on the edge of the bathtub, looking at the test result as if it had betrayed him. Maybe it's a false positive. That's a thing, isn't it? He was on his feet and halfway to the bedroom to get his keys to go get another one when a wave of nausea hit him and he raced back to the bathroom. He was able to calm his rolling stomach, splashing cold water on his face.

Who was he kidding? Of course he was pregnant. He was going to have a baby whose father won't even talk to him.

His head spun around crazily, thoughts flying on the wind with no order. He couldn't think straight.

On instinct, he went to the bedroom and called up his fathers. It was the weekend so they'd both be home.

"Hey, Chris," Colin said. He was always so cheerful, just hearing his voice actually did make Chris feel a little better.

"Hey. How's it going?"

Colin's cheerfulness disappeared. "What's up, son? You sound defeated."

It was always amazing to Chris how Colin was able to pick up on his moods just by a few words. "Things have been better."

"Do I need to go get Jeremy?"

"No…no reason to disturb him. I just…needed to hear a friendly voice."

Colin's silence on the other end was well-timed. Chris couldn't hold back as he explained everything that had happened since he last talked to them. To his credit, Chris didn't start crying, although the pressure of the tears behind his eyes threatened to overwhelm him.

"Oh, Chris, I'm so sorry he did that to you."

Chris sighed, squeezing at his eyes to make the pressure go away. "It's my own fault, I guess. I didn't think mentioning it was that important, but Landon thought differently. After I gave him such a hard time about not telling me about who he was..."

"Those are not equivalent," Colin said. "You did include it on your resume."

"Well, I downplayed it because, at the time, the experience, while it was a nice bit of money for an internship, didn't teach me much more than I already knew. I thought I was clear. I guess I wasn't." Chris stretched out on the bed, propped up against the headboard. "And now he won't return my calls, or texts, or emails. As far as I know, he hasn't even been back to the office. Oh God, Colin. I'm pregnant with his baby and I can't even tell him. What am I supposed to do now?"

"They haven't fired you yet, so just keep your head down and keep working. That will sort itself out. Obviously, you still have value to them or they would have escorted you out that Monday they talked to you. The truth will come out soon enough."

Colin's voice was reassuring, and Chris breathed through it, his heart slowing from the racing, panicked tempo that seemed to be the new normal lately.

"As for the baby," Colin continued, "we're a family, Chris. We take care of our family. We'll figure it out together, alright? And if you need to come home to regroup, Chris, that is okay. There's no shame in it. We will always have a place for all of you boys, no matter if you're grown with your own family. Come back and we'll work through this together."

Chris's throat closed up, choked from emotion. Colin and Jeremy were a godsend for him. They were there when there was no one else in Chris's life. They would be there for him now.

He let out a soft breath. "Thanks. I'll um...let me think about it and see how things progress at work."

"Alright. Do you want to talk to Jeremy?"

"Nah, if you could just catch him up, that'd be good. I have a ton of errands to run today so I should go."

"Of course. Love you, Chris. Don't forget it. You can always come home."

"Love you, Colin. Give my love to everyone."

Chris felt a little better after having talked to his father. Anything was better than feeling worse.

And laundry. He hated laundry.

He gathered his clothes and hauled them down to the basement to put the load on. While he waited through the wash cycle, his phone chimed with a notification. An email.

Opening it, it was a job pitch from a job recruiter. Well, wasn't that timely?

They were asking if he was still available for a job.

He scrolled up and expanded it to show the header information. The email was from Venandi Technology's HR department.

Chris tapped the phone against his chin. This was either a setup, or an honest to God opportunity. While his paranoia played merry havoc with his imagination that LeoTech's HR was setting him up, the header appeared to be real enough.

It was dangerous to accept the invitation for an interview. If it were a setup, he was hosed.

But he was already hosed where he was working. Chris knew the countdown had started against him.

There was no loyalty between him and LeoTech now. Certainly no loyalty to Landon, who wouldn't even acknowledge Chris existed.

Maybe…

Maybe this was the fresh start he needed.

He accepted the job interview time and hit send.

It was clear that he needed to move forward. Whatever happened, he was committed now.

Chapter 22 - Landon

The definition of insanity is doing the same thing expecting a different result. Landon, by this definition, was definitely verging on the edge of it. Or at least crazy.

He parked the Land Rover beneath a tree towards the edge of the parking lot at the park for shifters, just like he had done every night for the past month.

And just like every night for the past month, he shed his jacket and left the vehicle parked as he headed into the woods. There, he shifted into his lion form and planned to spend the next few hours running.

Not running anywhere or for any reason except one.

Running until he was exhausted was the only way he could get any sleep at night.

Sleeplessness plagued him until it was a constant companion, and it started the very night he threw Chris out of his apartment in a fit of stupid, prideful rage.

It was his punishment and his solace.

Punishment because running through the woods always brought back the memories of his run with Chris. The first time in Landon didn't know how long where he was full of life and love and desire. Where the pressures of his life fell away and all he needed he had in one man. How he had managed to screw that up with his unwillingness to trust his instincts, and his inability to set aside his anger and hear the man out.

Chris's tear-filled eyes haunted Landon in the deep of the night. Every time he closed his own eyes to get any sleep.

So he came back to the park at night as a reminder of what an idiot he was.

It was also his solace. It granted him a reprieve every night after the run, when he was bone-tired and ready to drop in exhaustion. Only then, his mind would wind down and allow him those few moments of sleep where he did not live the night over and over in his head.

He did enough of that during the day.

Taking off for the wood line at a run, Landon shifted on the move. Two feet hitting the ground, kicking up leaves, became four, and he disappeared into the brush to start his circuit of the park. Lately, it had taken five full laps for him to finally reach that state where he felt nothing.

Running at full speed, the world was a blur as it raced by. Branches whipped at his face and tangled in his mane. The leaves shuffled around his paws as he extended his claws to gain purchase on the ground to push faster. He rounded a corner, a small section of the lake where the trees encroached right up to the water, when a familiar whiff of cologne hit his nose.

Clint Knowles.

Landon slid to a stop, the water splashing around his paws, soaking the fur.

"You run like your tail's on fire," Clint's voice called out. "Or maybe running from a bad decision?"

He spun in place and saw his competitor. Clint stood in human form, watching as Landon waded out of the water. By the time Landon reached Clint, he was also in human form. "Usually, shifters come to the park to release their animal forms. It's kind of creepy to have you standing there in human spying on people. Oh, wait. You don't normally linger in the woods like a creep. You send your spies in."

"I appreciate your confidence in my ability to infiltrate your organization, Williams," Clint said. He pushed up from his lean, getting right up in Landon's personal space. At that distance, Clint's cologne drifted over him like a noxious cloud.

"Are you telling me you don't have your people working at LeoTech?"

"Most certainly not. But from what I'm hearing, you're sniffing around in the wrong places. I'm just saying. You may want to step up your screening process." Clint tapped firmly at Landon's chest. "Your heart gets in your way and you make careless decisions."

Landon slapped his hand away. "You talk a good game, but I have a hard time believing you're that deeply embedded. If you were deeper, you'd have done more damage."

Clint leaned in. "Oh, I've done exactly what I needed to do. And now I get to watch as you twist yourself in knots over it. Poor kitty."

"The problem with gloating—" Landon didn't finish his sentence before he shoved violently at Clint, taking him off his feet. Before Clint could roll out of the way, Landon shifted to his lion form. He pounced, teeth and claws out.

Clint's foot caught him in the gut and swept him off to the side. Landon landed on his side, then rolled to his paws. Clint shifted to lion and swiveled to meet Landon head-on as they charged at each other.

Rising onto his hind legs, Landon swiped with a massive paw, connecting with Clint's jaw. His claws raked along the tough hide. He intended to draw blood. Clint was a dangerous male. He was deliberately setting out to sabotage Landon, to take away what Landon was fighting so hard to protect. The security of his family's business.

Why Clint had decided to bring him down, Landon would never understand. He hadn't done anything to Clint when they were in college. Business was booming for their companies. There were more than enough client contacts to go around. So this repeated taunting, this pattern of behavior, made no sense to Landon.

He wasn't going to stand for it any longer.

They separated when Clint twisted out from beneath his paws and charged him. He bit into Landon's mane, trying to find skin and muscle to hold on. Landon rolled beneath Clint's body weight and dragged him down. They tumbled along down to the edge of the lake. Water splashed and the wet mud of the shoreline made gaining footing perilous. They flipped and turned, rolled and dragged as Landon continued to batter at Clint.

The scent of blood filled the air. Clint's claws had raked down Landon's side and the sting of the water was a reminder that they weren't testing each other's boundaries any longer. This was a full-on fight.

Landon was ready to meet that challenge.

His teeth sunk into the fleshy part of Clint's shoulder. Blood sprung out of the bite marks but Landon now had a firm hold on the other lion. He pulled, shook and dragged Clint as he struggled to get on his paws again. Landon kept him turned onto his back so Clint couldn't rise to his feet.

Holding to Clint now with his front paws, his teeth still firmly buried in Clint's shoulder he flipped them so Landon could kick at Clint's side with his back claws. Blood churned and mixed with the water.

Clint fell still beneath Landon's heavy body.

Defeat.

Landon waited for a moment to make sure it wasn't a trick before he released Clint and stepped back. The instant he let go, Clint shifted back to human. His normally immaculate suit was ripped and shredded, exposing the long gashes in his side. With a weak snarl, he struggled to his feet, gripping his injured shoulder.

He followed, inspecting the damage to his own clothing and body once fully human again.

They stood there, chests heaving, eyes flashing in the slowly fading light. Landon curled a lip in a snarl.

"This one goes to you, Williams," Clint said. He checked his shoulder. "But you don't win everything."

Landon spit at his feet.

"You see, I still get your Omega." Clint's smile was cruel. "You remember him, right? The one you dumped? The one your company shit on once word got out he was under review for being the 'spy'?"

Landon's heart clenched in his chest. "What are you talking about?"

Clint clucked his tongue and looked at Landon derisively. "Jesus, you can be so stupid. Chris Robertson. Once we heard about it, we rushed to get everything in order to offer him a new job. When he worked for us before, he wasn't all that notable. We go through interns like water so he didn't stand out. Competent was the best word we'd use. Then word got back that he had been having a bit of trouble at the company. So we used some strategic sleight of hand to point your HR in the direction we wanted them to go to cast doubt on Robertson. Knowing you like I do, I figured after casting suspicion on him, that meant you kicked him out of your bed, too. What better way to destabilize you than to take what was yours."

He ran his hand through his hair and tried to salvage his suit, giving it up for a lost cause. Clint hadn't lost any of his arrogance. "So, sure, you win this fight. But I win the prize. An Omega that used to be yours. That *you* willingly let go."

Landon's blood rushed through his ears. He closed his eyes to keep his desire to punch Clint's smug face until it was a ruin.

When he opened them again, Clint was gone.

Chapter 23 - Chris

"When was the last time you wore this suit?"

Max circled around Chris, tugging at the jacket. Chris had to suck his stomach in to get it to button.

"When I interviewed for the position at LeoTech." He looked at his reflection with dismay. Already he was putting on weight. It wasn't a lot and he wasn't actually *showing* or anything.

The suit was a lot snugger than he was comfortable with.

"Maybe you can get away with not buttoning it," Max said as he stepped back to inspect Chris.

"I suppose I could." Chris slid his thumb beneath the waistband and shook his head. "It feels like it's cutting me in half."

Max swatted his hand. "It doesn't look it. You look fine. You're just a little nervous. That's all."

"More than a little." Chris sighed and unbuckled the belt and slid it from the loops. "I have a lot riding on this interview tomorrow."

"So you're really going through with it?" Max flopped onto Chris's bed and leaned back. "You had just started gaining traction at this place."

"I really don't feel like I have a choice." He unbuttoned his slacks and blew out a breath. "Maybe I can keep from busting a button until the interview is done."

"We can always move the button." Max reached out and tugged at it. "Your belt will cover it. Do you have needle and thread?"

"Like Colin would let me leave home without a full sewing kit?" Chris dug around in the top of his closet. "I'm hoping I can make comparable money at Venandi. When I interned there, the pay wasn't all that great."

"Why not go in and talk to your boss and explain things again? Tell him that Venandi is trying to poach you away but you don't want to go because you really *like* working there?"

"I'm not so sure I like working there any more, Max." Chris found the kit and pulled it down. A few of his folded winter clothes tumbled out on top of him and he pushed them away, letting them fall to the floor. He stepped over them to take the kit to the bed and he flopped it open. "Can I be loyal to a company who has shown no loyalty to me? Who's willing to hang me out before even hearing my side?"

Max fished around and pulled out the seam ripper to cut the button off. "Are you talking about the company or its CEO?"

Chris flinched. Max had sliced right to the bone and he didn't mean the button. "He wouldn't even listen."

"Here." Max handed him the needle and thread. "Have you told him you're pregnant?"

"And when was I going to do that? He's ghosted on me. Sometimes…" Chris squeezed his eyes shut to keep the tears from coming. He'd done enough crying over the Alpha. It was time to get past it.

Which was hard even on his best days. Memories of Landon filled every spare moment of thought. "Sometimes I catch his scent. I know he's been in the building. But I never see him. Of course, no one's talking to me beyond expected niceties. I don't even get good gossip about where he's at or how he's doing."

He shook his head, focusing on getting the needle threaded for Max while he cleaned the button up and futzed with the waistband to find a good place to reattach it. "Doesn't matter. It's better this way. The last thing I want is to make him madder by giving him a reason to think I'm entrapping him."

"Saints preserve me from a bad romance," Max said. He took the needle from Chris and stitched the button a few times to hold it so Chris could test the position when they buttoned it up. "You can't *not* tell him."

"Maybe. I need to get away from the company. It's soured now. Some distance is needed or I'll just collapse like a house of cards."

Max motioned for Chris to look in the mirror to test the fit. "Have you considered coming home?"

Chris examined how the slacks fastened. It wasn't optimal but it would have to do. He stripped the slacks off and handed them to Max. "I have and I'm not. I can do this. I can survive on my own. And I can be a single parent."

"That's just it, Chris; you don't *have* to."

"I want to." Chris sat next to his foster brother. They had been raised together, and of all of his other brothers, he was closest to Max. "And I know I have a safety net if I fail utterly."

"That's just it. You won't." Max hissed a breath and shook his finger out after he poked himself with the needle. "That's what makes you so strong."

Chris looked down at his hands and he clasped them together. "I don't feel particularly strong at the moment. I'm scared shitless."

"You wear it well." Max knotted the thread and clipped the excess. "Just like you'll wear these. Here; try them on with the belt."

While Chris slipped the slacks on, fastened them and then slid the belt through the loops, Max put the sewing kit back together. Max joined him at the mirror and nodded in approval. "I can't tell."

"I can but it'll do. Thanks."

Max settled a hand on Chris's shoulder. "That's what family does. Now, I need to get out of here. I promised some buddies we'd meet for drinks downtown. Are you going to be okay?"

They walked to the front door. Chris pulled Max in for a hug and his brother's solid arms wrapped around him. "We all love you, Christopher Robertson. If anyone can pull this off, you can."

Chris slapped his shoulder and stepped back. "Thanks."

"Alright. Seriously, don't be a stranger. Colin and Jeremy want you to come home at some point. Don't disappoint them." Max pulled the door open to step through.

"I promise I won—"

Chris almost ran into Max when his brother stopped in the doorway. "Uh, hello," Max said.

"Is Chris here?"

That was Landon's voice. Chris's mouth went dry and his face drained of all blood. Landon?

"Landon?"

Max turned to meet Chris's gaze, a silent 'do I need to take out the trash' expression on his face.

"Chris." Landon sounded relieved. "I need to talk to you." He stopped, his attention shifting between Chris and Max. "Please."

Chris smiled at Max and nodded. "Okay. Max, I'll call you tomorrow."

Max pressed his lips together. "You better." He stepped into the hall, gave Landon the best stink eye in the world and then disappeared.

"My brother," Chris said. Not that he owed Landon an explanation of anything. "Come in."

Now that Max was out of his way, Chris realized that Landon was in a pretty sorry state. He had scratches on his face and his hair was tangled and filled with twigs and leaves. His clothes were a muddy, scratched up mess.

It was the look in his eyes that gave Chris pause.

Those were not the eyes of anger.

Chapter 24 - Landon

The Alpha in Landon rose up in protest when he saw another man in Chris's apartment. The scent told him it was another Omega but that didn't make him any less threatening. To find out he was Chris's brother was a huge relief. Maybe he hadn't so thoroughly screwed this up.

He stepped to the side and waited for Chris to close the door. Chris stood there, his hands in his pockets. He was dressed in slacks and a t-shirt. His feet were bare.

"Were you going somewhere?" Landon asked. "I didn't mean to interrupt—"

"No. I was making sure I am ready...for tomorrow."

Chris shifted from foot to foot. He was nervous about something. He wouldn't meet Landon's gaze.

"Don't go."

"What?" Chris's head snapped up with a mixed expression Landon couldn't read.

"Don't go. To the interview. Tomorrow. I know you have an interview with Venandi. I'm asking you please to not go."

The silence was maddening. He couldn't read Chris or what was going through his mind. Landon felt the rising anxiety in his chest. Had he let this go on too long that now the Omega was going to reject him?

"I screwed up, Chris. I screwed up so much and I know it now. I knew it that night when you…when I threw you out. I was…I can't even begin to describe it." Landon couldn't keep still. He had to move or he'd go mad.

He started to pace in front of Chris. "You're all I think about. You're all I dream about. You're all I want. You're all I need. I don't want anyone else. You're mine and I knew it the first day I saw you. And I was stupid to even think for a *minute* that you had betrayed me. Because I know better. *I know better* and I let my anger get the better of me instead of letting you explain."

Landon risked stepping up close to Chris, gingerly placing his hands on the Omega's arms. He inhaled. Chris smelled different.

Not different like he'd been with someone else.

Of course, Landon would have no right to be upset if Chris had been claimed by a new Alpha. It was a scent he couldn't place but Chris's body chemistry had changed.

"I know you're not the spy. HR is wrong. They have it wrong and first thing in the morning, I'll fix this. I swear I'll fix this so please… don't go tomorrow. I love you. Stay with me. Be my mate. I want to be your Alpha. I know making it on your own is important to you and I promise, I *promise* I won't get in the way of that. You can have a career, doing anything you want, just don't go to Venan—"

Then, just that quickly, Chris's mouth was on his, kissing the rest of his words away. Everything focused down to where their lips touched, and Landon felt a great weight lift off his chest.

Chris broke contact with a soft gasp. "Okay."

Okay. *Okay*. Landon's relief washed over him like a warm rain.

"You're such a doofus," Chris said. He slid his arms around Landon's waist to hug him. "I love you, too. I have almost from the start."

Landon gathered him up and held him close. "Thank you. I'm sorry. Chris, God, I am so sorry."

"Shut up already. I understand. I was pretty miserable without you, too." Chris stepped back from Landon's embrace until he was arm's length away. Landon didn't like that. He wanted Chris back in his arms, where he belonged. "Now I feel like I'm going to screw this up again."

"You weren't the one who screwed this up—"

Chris held his hand out for Landon to stop talking. He mashed his lips together to allow Chris to say whatever he had to say.

"Landon...remember when we had sex at the park?"

"It's all I dream about."

Chris laughed softly. "Yeah, me too. But...do you remember that we didn't use a condom that night?"

Landon nodded quickly. "I do."

When Chris swallowed hard, it began to dawn on Landon *why* Chris smelled differently. "Oh. Oh, you're...oh."

"Yep. Pregnant. I wanted to tell you. I did. I didn't want to keep this a secret, but you weren't returning my calls..."

None of that mattered to Landon. He had been the stupid one. "You're going to have my baby," he said softly. "Mine. My baby. For me."

Chris looked up through his bangs, so uncertain and so amazing attractive that Landon fought between warring desires to kiss the uncertainty away and to drag the man to the bedroom and fuck him senseless into the mattress. "You're not mad?"

"Mad? Why would I be...Chris, this is amazing news." Landon stepped forward swiftly and lifted Chris in his arms to swing him around. "My baby. My Omega is having my baby."

"*Your* Omega?" Chris asked.

Landon stopped spinning. "Mine," he said definitively. "If you'll have me."

Chapter 25 - Chris

Chris held on to Landon, dangling in his embrace with his feet off the floor. It mirrored how he felt inside. Lifted up and floating above the ground. Held there, supported by the man he loved.

He carefully pushed Landon's tangled hair from the Alpha's face and gazed into the honey-colored eyes.

Love reflected back to him. It wrapped them in a cloak of fierce protectiveness.

His Alpha.

Landon was giving himself to Chris. Never in a million years had he expected this turn of events. The map he had for his life was nothing like the reality staring at him.

Cupping Landon's face, he dipped in for a soft brush of lips. It quickly turned heated as Landon stretched to meet him, taking Chris's mouth in hungry kisses. Chris wrapped his legs around Landon's waist and threw himself, heart and soul, into it. Need, desire, lust, love. It was all one mixed, tangled bag of emotions that felt right when he held it for Landon.

"You need," Chris panted out when he broke their kiss, "to take me to bed right now."

Landon smiled and stole another kiss. "I've been wanting to do that since I got here."

Chris looked at him with one eyebrow lifted. "And we're still standing here."

With a laugh, Landon looked around Chris and headed for the obvious hallway. "I've never been in your apartment before."

"At the end of the hall," Chris said before diving in to silence Landon talking. Talking was done. He needed to taste Landon. His kisses, like his hair, were wild, flying in the wind. Chris's toes curled from the kiss.

Chris spared a moment for embarrassment that he hadn't made his bed up that morning. It quickly dissolved under the realization that before they were done, it'd be messed up anyway.

Hopefully, ending with Landon staying the night.

Landon stretched him out on the mattress, braced over him.

Covered and shielded, Chris, for the first time in his life, felt as if someone would protect him from all the storms of life. His fathers were good men and they took in lost boys to help give them stability in a world that was rocked with such instability.

It obviously wasn't the same. Now, Landon was here, the physical promise that he would care and love for Chris like no other.

His body tingled from head to foot.

Landon eased his body weight down to pin Chris to the bed. He brushed at the bonding spot on Chris's neck. "I want this, Chris."

Just the brush of his fingertips sent waves of sensation over Chris and all he could do was cry out softly. "Please. I do too, so just…please. Now. Please."

Landon laughed softly and brushed their mouths together. "And I guess we don't need to worry about condoms." He paused, a look of concern on his face. "It won't do anything to the baby?"

"You're adorable," Chris said with a soft snicker. "It won't."

He pushed at Landon so the Alpha would rise to his knees. With impatient tugging, he worked Landon's jeans open and reached in to palm at his cock. Landon gasped, his head dropping and his hips bucking forward into his grip. It hardened completely under his attention. Chris's twitched in response.

Landon shifted off the bed to tear at his clothing. Chris followed suit, unable to focus when Landon stood there in perfect Alpha form. The Alpha was a model of physical perfection.

Leaving their clothing in scattered piles on the floor, Landon crawled across the bed, stalking Chris and causing him to back up until his head rested on the pillow. He pulled Chris's leg up, bending it at the knee and holding it in place with his shoulder. It opened Chris, leaving him vulnerable to Landon's probing. "I'll never get tired of this," Landon whispered between kisses along Chris's collar bone. "How you're always so wet for me."

Chris could come just from Landon's talented fingers. The man touched in him in ways so intimate it was dizzying. Frightening. Amazing.

Slow kisses as Landon's fingers worked into him drove Chris to the brink of insanity. He wiggled, Landon's dick, hard and dripping precome against his stretched out thigh. "Landon," he whined.

Landon nipped playfully at his collarbone before he pulled his fingers and shifted his weight to keep Chris's leg hitched up to position his cock at Chris's hole.

Chris needed to feel Landon filling him and he shifted impatiently. For God's sake, the man was driving him crazy. "Let me turn over."

"No," Landon said. The word was authoritative and final. "I want to watch your face when you come."

With one masterful stroke, his cockhead popped past Chris's muscle. One of them gasped. Maybe both of them. Chris saw stars for a moment, but it wasn't from pain.

It was something more profound.

He forced his eyes open to catch and hold Landon's as the Alpha slid completely into him. Taking his full length, Chris was finally able to breathe. He panted softly, craning his neck to steal kisses as Landon slowly worked up his thrusts until the bed squeaked and Chris rocked beneath the motion.

Every thrust was nirvana for Chris. Torn between closing his eyes and riding the wave and keeping his gaze locked with Landon's, eventually that option was taken from him.

Landon ducked, lapping with a soft, wet tongue over his bond sight. Primitive arousal and need spiked with every lick. His tempo picked up until his thrusts were short and hard as he plowed Chris. Tongue was replaced with teeth as they lightly scraped his skin.

Chris arched beneath Landon with a surprised cry as it translated through his body at the speed of light, setting every nerve on fire.

A puff of air on his throat was the final nail in his coffin as Landon latched down on the spot.

Chris's world exploded behind his eyes in magnificent colors. He was on fire. It consumed him from the inside. Losing track of everything, a cry tore from his throat, keening and remarkably sounding like Landon's name. Landon's answering growl set everything into perfect focus.

Without being touched, Chris's orgasm pulsed from him, warm and slick against his skin. Landon gasped, finally releasing the bond spot as his body also shook before he stopped thrusting. Vaguely, Chris was aware of the throbbing of Landon's cock.

Landon collapsed on top of him, clumsily pushing Chris's leg so he could lower it. It fell to the mattress with an undignified flop.

The stars finally started to clear from his eyes. The bond spot throbbed now and he risked touching at it. It didn't feel any different beneath his fingers but it felt hot to him under the skin. He glanced up to see Landon smiling down at him.

He smiled back.

"All mine," Landon said. He shifted a little to make room to run his hand along Chris's stomach, smearing the cooling come over his skin. "Mine, too."

"Definitely yours, too."

Silent for a moment longer, Landon kissed Chris tenderly before he got comfortable again, still embraced between Chris's spread legs. He braced on his elbows and stole kisses, which Chris gladly indulged.

Landon nuzzled at Chris's jaw and kissed his temple. "Do you need to call to cancel the interview?" His arms tightening indicated he actually didn't want Chris to get up at all.

Chris thought about it before he shook his head. He burrowed closer against Landon. The job wasn't necessary any longer. Not that leaving LeoTech wasn't the right choice. Going to Venandi wasn't a solution. Some decisions still needed to be made.

Right at that moment? Not a priority.

"Nah. I'm sure they'll will figure it out."

Epilogue - Landon

The sun was going down as Landon pulled into the driveway.

His new driveway. In front of his new house.

With the addition of a baby, Landon was resolved his son would have a backyard to play in. Chris's old apartment and his penthouse had no safe places to raise a baby.

The realtor sign was leaning against the garage door. He'd call in the morning to make sure they came to get it or he'd dump it in the garbage because this house was now his.

Just like Chris was his and just like their baby was his.

Landon found he liked having things that were his. It even spurred him to start taking a more active role in the company.

He dragged the few groceries he picked up on the way home inside and put them away. Further into the house, he could hear Chris singing softly. So he was home and the nanny was gone for the day.

Once everything was settled, he glanced through the mail on his way down the hall.

The singing grew louder.

Stopping at the door, he leaned against it and took in the scene.

Chris had insisted on getting the huge, wooden rocker. It was a good purchase. Both of them spent many late nights in it, nursing an energetic baby.

Landon didn't recognize the tune Chris was humming but it was pleasant all the same. He could see that Caleb was being lulled to sleep by it. "You have the magic touch."

"Is it magic when it's the same song I hear over and over again on one of Caleb's favorite shows?" Caleb looked up at Landon and smiled.

Parenthood definitely suited Chris. He glowed like he'd never seen any one person before.

"Every time I see you," Landon said softly, "I fall in love with you all over again. Whether it's with a coffee from a vendor or with twigs in your hair or your face slick with sweat and you're swearing to never get pregnant again and would someone please get this—"

"Alright, alright." Chris shook his head with a laugh. "It was the drugs talking, okay?"

"So you're open to having more babies?" Landon dropped the mail on the changing table and went to kneel next to Chris.

"Not right now, no. I just started this job. I'd like to keep it for a while this time."

Landon gave a dramatic sigh. "Fine. How's it going, anyway?"

"It's small. A really small indie conservation company. We do double duty in many positions. It's challenging, exhausting and...a perfect fit."

Picking up the half sleeping baby's hand, Landon marveled at how tiny it was in relation to his finger. A thrill shot through him when Caleb closed his fist around it. "You could have stayed at LeoTech. Everything got worked out and they found the person responsible for all the trouble."

"Not in good conscience. Being the mate of the CEO? It isn't a good look. Claims of nepotism and favoritism? No, thanks. Besides...I think I was born to be exactly where I am now."

Landon's pride swelled. He brushed his fingers lightly through Chris's hair. "Chris. I have something on my mind."

Chris's eyebrows lifted and he gave Landon his attention.

Looking at those lovely brown eyes...there was no doubt or reluctance when Chris looked at him. This was the right decision.

"Marry me."

Chris's lips parted on a gasp and he stopped rocking. Looking down at their baby boy and then back up at Landon, a wide smile broke out across his face. "Yes. Yes I will."

Surging up for a kiss, contentment settled over Landon.

His life finally had order, meaning, purpose.

He had Chris and a family. There was no better purpose than that.

Printed in Poland
by Amazon Fulfillment
Poland Sp. z o.o., Wrocław